Penguin Books
Much Obliged, Jeeves

Pelham Grenville Wodehouse was born in 1881 in Guildford,
the son of a civil servant, and educated at Dulwich College. He
spent a brief period working for the Hong Kong and Shanghai
Bank before abandoning finance for writing, earning a living by
journalism and selling stories to magazines.

An enormously popular and prolific writer, he produced
about a hundred books. In Jeeves, the ever resourceful
'gentleman's personal gentleman', and the good-hearted young
blunderer Bertie Wooster, he created two of the best-known and
best-loved characters in twentieth-century literature. Their
exploits, first collected in *Carry on, Jeeves*, were chronicled in
fourteen books, and have been repeatedly adapted for television,
radio and the stage. Wodehouse also created many other comic
figures, notably Lord Emsworth, the Hon. Galahad
Threepwood, Psmith and the numerous members of the Drones
Club. He was part-author and writer of fifteen straight plays
and of 250 lyrics for some thirty musical comedies. *The Times*
hailed him as a 'comic genius recognized in his lifetime as a
classic and an old master of farce'.

P. G. Wodehouse said, 'I believe there are two ways of
writing novels. One is mine, making a sort of musical comedy
without music and ignoring real life altogether; the other is
going right deep down into life and not caring a damn.'

Wodehouse married in 1914 and took American citizenship
in 1955. He was created a Knight of the British Empire in the
1975 New Year's Honours List. In a BBC interview he said that
he had no ambitions left now that he had been knighted and
there was a waxwork of him in Madame Tussaud's. He died on
St Valentine's Day, 1975, at the age of ninety-three.

P. G. Wodehouse published and forthcoming in Penguin

P. G. Wodehouse
Much Obliged, Jeeves

P.G.Wodehouse

Much Obliged, Jeeves

PENGUIN BOOKS

PENGUIN BOOKS

Published by the Penguin Group
Penguin Books Ltd, 27 Wrights Lane, London w8 5tz, England
Penguin Putnam Inc., 375 Hudson Street, New York, New York 10014, USA
Penguin Books Australia Ltd, Ringwood, Victoria, Australia
Penguin Books Canada Ltd, 10 Alcorn Avenue, Toronto, Ontario, Canada m4v 3b2
Penguin Books (NZ) Ltd, Private Bag 102902, NSMC, Auckland, New Zealand

Penguin Books Ltd, Registered Offices: Harmondsworth, Middlesex, England

First published in Great Britain by Barrie and Jenkins Ltd 1971
Published in Penguin Books 1981
10

Set in 9/11pt Monotype Trump
Typeset by Rowland Phototypesetting Ltd,
Bury St Edmunds, Suffolk
Printed in England by Clays Ltd, St Ives plc

As I slid into my chair at the breakfast table and started to deal with the toothsome eggs and bacon which Jeeves had given of his plenty, I was conscious of a strange exhilaration, if I've got the word right. Pretty good the set-up looked to me. Here I was, back in the old familiar headquarters, and the thought that I had seen the last of Totleigh Towers, of Sir Watkyn Bassett, of his daughter Madeline and above all of the unspeakable Spode, or Lord Sidcup as he now calls himself, was like the medium dose for adults of one of those patent medicines which tone the system and impart a gentle glow.

'These eggs, Jeeves,' I said. 'Very good. Very tasty.'

'Yes, sir?'

'Laid, no doubt, by contented hens. And the coffee, perfect. Nor must I omit to give a word of praise to the bacon. I wonder if you notice anything about me this morning.'

'You seem in good spirits, sir.'

'Yes, Jeeves, I am happy today.'

'I am very glad to hear it, sir.'

'You might say I'm sitting on top of the world with a rainbow round my shoulder.'

'A most satisfactory state of affairs, sir.'

'What's the word I've heard you use from time to time – begins with eu?'

'Euphoria, sir?'

'That's the one. I've seldom had a sharper attack of euphoria. I feel full to the brim of Vitamin B. Mind you, I don't know how long it will last. Too often it is when one feels fizziest that the storm clouds begin doing their stuff.'

'Very true, sir. Full many a glorious morning have I seen flatter the mountain tops with sovereign eye, kissing with golden face the meadows green, gilding pale streams with heavenly alchemy, Anon permit the basest clouds to ride with ugly rack on his celestial face and from the forlorn world his visage hide, stealing unseen to west with this disgrace.'

'Exactly,' I said. I couldn't have put it better myself. 'One always has to budget for a change in the weather. Still, the thing to do is to keep on being happy while you can.'

'Precisely, sir. *Carpe diem*, the Roman poet Horace advised. The English poet Herrick expressed the same sentiment when he suggested that we should gather rosebuds while we may. Your elbow is in the butter, sir.'

'Oh, thank you, Jeeves.'

Well, all right so far. Off to a nice start. But now we come to something which gives me pause. In recording the latest instalment of the Bertram Wooster Story, a task at which I am about to have a pop, I don't see how I can avoid delving into the past a good deal, touching on events which took place in previous instalments, and explaining who's who and what happened when and where and why, and this will make it heavy going for those who have been with me from the start. 'Old hat' they will cry or, if French, '*Déjà vu*'.

On the other hand, I must consider the new customers. I can't just leave the poor perishers to try to puzzle things out for themselves. If I did, the exchanges in the present case would run somewhat as follows.

SELF: The relief I felt at having escaped from Totleigh Towers was stupendous.
NEW C: What's Totleigh Towers?

SELF: For one thing it had looked odds on that I
          should have to marry Madeline.

NEW C: Who's Madeline?

SELF: Gussie Fink-Nottle, you see, had eloped with
          the cook.

NEW C: Who's Gussie Fink-Nottle?

SELF: But most fortunately Spode was in the offing
          and scooped her up, saving me from the
          scaffold.

NEW C: Who's Spode?

You see. Hopeless. Confusion would be rife, as one
might put it. The only way out that I can think of is to
ask the old gang to let their attention wander for a bit –
there are heaps of things they can be doing; washing the
car, solving the crossword puzzle, taking the dog for a
run – while I place the facts before the newcomers.

Briefly, then, owing to circumstances I needn't go
into, Madeline Bassett daughter of Sir Watkyn Bassett of
Totleigh Towers, Glos. had long been under the
impression that I was hopelessly in love with her and
had given to understand that if ever she had occasion to
return her betrothed, Gussie Fink-Nottle, to store, she
would marry me. Which wouldn't have fitted in with
my plans at all, she though physically in the pin-up
class, being as mushy a character as ever broke biscuit,
convinced that the stars are God's daisy chain and that
every time a fairy blows its wee nose a baby is born. The
last thing, as you can well imagine, one would want
about the home.

So when Gussie unexpectedly eloped with the cook,
it looked as though Bertram was for it. If a girl thinks
you're in love with her and says she will marry you, you
can't very well voice a preference for being dead in a
ditch. Not, I mean, if you want to regard yourself as a
preux chevalier, as the expression is, which is always
my aim.

But just as I was about to put in my order for
sackcloth and ashes, up, as I say, popped Spode, now
going about under the alias of Lord Sidcup. He had loved
her since she was so high but had never got around to
mentioning it, and when he did so now, they clicked
immediately. And the thought that she was safely out of
circulation and no longer a menace was possibly the
prime ingredient in my current euphoria.

I think that makes everything clear to the meanest
intelligence, does it not? Right ho, so we can go ahead.
Where were we? Ah yes, I had just told Jeeves that I was
sitting on top of the world with a rainbow round my
shoulder, but expressing a doubt as to whether this state
of things would last, and how well-founded that doubt
proved to be; for scarcely a forkful of eggs and b later it
was borne in upon me that life was not the grand sweet
song I had supposed it to be, but, as you might say, stern
and earnest and full of bumps.

'Was I mistaken, Jeeves,' I said, making idle
conversation as I sipped my coffee, 'or as the mists of
sleep shredded away this morning did I hear your
typewriter going?'

'Yes, sir. I was engaged in composition.'

'A dutiful letter to Charlie Silversmith?' I said,
alluding to his uncle who held the post of butler at
Deverill Hall, where we had once been pleasant visitors.
'Or possibly a lyric in the manner of the bloke who
advocates gathering rosebuds?'

'Neither, sir. I was recording the recent happenings at
Totleigh Towers for the club book.'

And here, dash it, I must once more ask what I may
call the old sweats to let their attention wander while I
put the new arrivals abreast.

Jeeves, you must know (I am addressing the new
arrivals), belongs to a club for butlers and gentlemen's
gentlemen round Curzon Street way, and one of the
rules there is that every member must contribute to the

club book the latest information concerning the fellow he's working for, the idea being to inform those seeking employment of the sort of thing they will be taking on. If a member is contemplating signing up with someone, he looks him up in the club book, and if he finds that he puts out crumbs for the birdies every morning and repeatedly saves golden-haired children from being run over by automobiles, he knows he is on a good thing and has no hesitation in accepting office. Whereas if the book informs him that the fellow habitually kicks starving dogs and generally begins the day by throwing the breakfast porridge at his personal attendant, he is warned in time to steer clear of him.

Which is all very well and one follows the train of thought, but in my opinion such a book is pure dynamite and ought not to be permitted. There are, Jeeves has informed me, eleven pages in it about me; and what will the harvest be, I ask him, if it falls into the hands of my Aunt Agatha, with whom my standing is already low. She spoke her mind freely enough some years ago when – against my personal wishes – I was found with twenty-three cats in my bedroom and again when I was accused – unjustly, I need hardly say – of having marooned A. B. Filmer, the Cabinet minister, on an island in her lake. To what heights of eloquence would she not soar, if informed of my vicissitudes at Totleigh Towers? The imagination boggles, Jeeves, I tell him.

To which he replies that it won't fall into the hands of my Aunt Agatha, she not being likely to drop in at the Junior Ganymede, which is what his club is called, and there the matter rests. His reasoning is specious and he has more or less succeeded in soothing my tremors, but I still can't help feeling uneasy, and my manner, as I addressed him now, had quite a bit of agitation in it.

'Good Lord!' I ejaculated, if ejaculated is the word I want. 'Are you really writing up that Totleigh business?'

'Yes, sir.'

'All the stuff about my being supposed to have pinched old Bassett's amber statuette?'

'Yes, sir.'

'And the night I spent in a prison cell? Is this necessary? Why not let the dead past bury its dead? Why not forget all about it?'

'Impossible, sir.'

'Why impossible? Don't tell me you can't forget things. You aren't an elephant.'

I thought I had him there, but no.

'It is my membership in the Junior Ganymede which restrains me from obliging you, sir. The rules with reference to the club book are very strict and the penalty for omitting to contribute to it severe. Actual expulsion has sometimes resulted.'

'I see,' I said. I could appreciate that this put him in quite a spot, the feudal spirit making him wish to do the square thing by the young master, while a natural disinclination to get bunged out of a well-loved club urged him to let the young master boil his head. The situation seemed to me to call for what is known as a compromise.

'Well, couldn't you water the thing down a bit? Omit one or two of the juiciest episodes?'

'I fear not, sir. The full facts are required. The committee insists on this.'

I suppose I ought not at this point to have expressed a hope that his blasted committee would trip over banana skins and break their ruddy necks, for I seemed to detect on his face a momentary look of pain. But he was broadminded and condoned it.

'Your chagrin does not surprise me, sir. One can, however, understand their point of view. The Junior Ganymede club book is a historic document. It has been in existence more than eighty years.'

'It must be the size of a house.'

'No, sir, the records are in several volumes. The present one dates back some twelve years. And one must remember that it is not every employer who demands a great deal of space.'

'Demands!'

'I should have said "requires". As a rule, a few lines suffice. Your eighteen pages are quite exceptional.'

'Eighteen? I thought it was eleven.'

'You are omitting to take into your calculations the report of your misadventures at Totleigh Towers, which I have nearly completed. I anticipate that this will run to approximately seven. If you will permit me, sir, I will pat your back.'

He made this kindly offer because I had choked on a swallow of coffee. A few pats and I was myself again and more than a little incensed, as always happens when we are discussing his literary work. Eighteen pages, I mean to say, and every page full of stuff calculated, if thrown open to the public, to give my prestige the blackest of eyes. Conscious of a strong desire to kick the responsible parties in the seat of the pants, I spoke with a generous warmth.

'Well, I call it monstrous. There's no other word for it. Do you know what that blasted committee of yours are inviting? Blackmail, that's what they're inviting. Let some man of ill will get his hooks on that book, and what'll be the upshot? Ruin, Jeeves, that's what'll be the upshot.'

I don't know if he drew himself to his full height, because I was lighting a cigarette at the moment and wasn't looking, but I think he must have done, for his voice, when he spoke, was the chilly voice of one who has drawn himself to his full height.

'There are no men of ill will in the Junior Ganymede, sir.'

I contested this statement hotly.

'That's what *you* think. How about Brinkley?' I said,

my allusion being to a fellow the agency had sent me some years previously when Jeeves and I had parted company temporarily because he didn't like me playing the banjolele. 'He's a member, isn't he?'

'A county member, sir. He rarely comes to the club. In passing, sir, his name is not Brinkley, it is Bingley.'

I waved an impatient cigarette holder. I was in no mood to split straws. Or is it hairs?

'His name is not of the essence, Jeeves. What *is* of the e is that he went off on his afternoon out, came back in an advanced state of intoxication, set the house on fire and tried to dismember me with a carving knife.'

'A most unpleasant experience, sir.'

'Having heard noises down below, I emerged from my room and found him wrestling with the grandfather clock, with which he appeared to have had a difference. He then knocked over a lamp and leaped up the stairs at me, complete with cutlass. By a miracle I avoided becoming the late Bertram Wooster, but only by a miracle. And you say there are no men of ill will in the Junior Ganymede club. Tchah!' I said. It is an expression I don't often use, but the situation seemed to call for it.

Things had become difficult. Angry passions were rising and dudgeon bubbling up a bit. It was fortunate that at this juncture the telephone should have tootled, causing a diversion.

'Mrs Travers, sir,' said Jeeves, having gone to the instrument.

2

I had already divined who was at the other end of the wire, my good and deserving Aunt Dahlia having a habit of talking on the telephone with the breezy vehemence of a hog-caller in the western states of America calling his hogs to come and get it. She got this way through hunting a lot in her youth with the Quorn and the Pytchley. What with people riding over hounds and hounds taking time off to chase rabbits, a girl who hunts soon learns to make herself audible. I believe that she, when in good voice, could be heard in several adjoining counties.

I stepped to the telephone, well pleased. There are few males or females whose society I enjoy more than that of this genial sister of my late father, and it was quite a time since we had foregathered. She lives near the town of Market Snodsbury in Worcestershire and sticks pretty closely to the rural seat, while I, as Jeeves had just recorded in the club book, had had my time rather full elsewhere of late. I was smiling sunnily as I took up the receiver. Not much good, of course, as she couldn't see me, but it's the spirit that counts.

'Hullo, aged relative.'

'Hullo to you, you young blot. Are you sober?'

I felt a natural resentment at being considered capable of falling under the influence of the sauce at ten in the morning, but I reminded myself that aunts will be aunts. Show me an aunt, I've often said, and I will show you someone who doesn't give a hoot how much her *obiter dicta* may wound a nephew's sensibilities. With a touch

of hauteur I reassured her on the point she had raised
and asked her in what way I could serve her.

'How about lunch?'

'I'm not in London. I'm at home. And you can serve
me, as you call it, by coming here. Today, if possible.'

'Your words are music to my ears, old ancestor.
Nothing could tickle me pinker,' I said, for I am always
glad to accept her hospitality and to renew my
acquaintance with the unbeatable eatables dished up by
her superb French chef Anatole, God's gift to the gastric
juices. I have often regretted that I have but one stomach
to put at his disposal. 'Staying how long?'

'As long as you like, my beamish boy. I'll let you
know when the time comes to throw you out. The great
thing is to get you here.'

I was touched, as who would not have been, by the
eagerness she showed for my company. Too many of my
circle are apt when inviting me to their homes to stress
the fact that they are only expecting me for the
week-end and to dwell with too much enthusiasm on
the excellence of the earlier trains back to the
metropolis on Monday morning. The sunny smile
widened an inch or two.

'Awfully good of you to have me, old blood relation.'

'It is, rather.'

'I look forward to seeing you.'

'Who wouldn't?'

'Èach minute will seem like an hour till we meet.
How's Anatole?'

'Greedy young pig, always thinking of Anatole.'

'Difficult to help it. The taste lingers. How is his art
these days?'

'At its peak.'

'That's good.'

'Ginger says his output has been a revelation to
him.'

I asked her to repeat this. It had sounded to me

just as if she had said 'Ginger says his output has been a revelation to him', and I knew this couldn't be the case. It turned out, however, that it was.

'Ginger?' I said, not abreast.

'Harold Winship. He told me to call him Ginger. He's staying here. He says he's a friend of yours, which he would scarcely admit unless he knew it could be proved against him. You do know him, don't you? He speaks of having been at Oxford with you.'

I uttered a joyful cry, and she said if I did it again, she would sue me, it having nearly cracked her eardrum. A notable instance of the pot calling the kettle black, as the old saying has it, she having been cracking mine since the start of the proceedings.

'Know him?' I said. 'You bet I know him. We were like . . . Jeeves!'

'Sir?'

'Who were those two fellows?'

'Sir?'

'Greek, if I remember correctly. Always mentioned when the subject of bosom pals comes up.'

'Would you be referring to Damon and Pythias, sir?'

'That's right. We were like Damon and Pythias, old ancestor. But what's he doing *chez* you? I wasn't aware that you and he had ever met.'

'We hadn't. But his mother was an old school friend of mine.'

'I see.'

'And when I heard he was standing for Parliament in the by-election at Market Snodsbury, I wrote to him and told him to make my house his base. Much more comfortable than dossing at a pub.'

'Oh, you've got a by-election at Market Snodsbury, have you?'

'Under full steam.'

'And Ginger's one of the candidates?'

'The Conservative one. You seem surprised.'

'I am. You might say stunned. I wouldn't have thought it was his dish at all. How's he doing?'

'Difficult to say so far. Anyway, he needs all the help he can get, so I want you to come and canvass for him.'

This made me chew the lower lip for a moment. One has to exercise caution at a time like this, or where is one?

'What does it involve?' I asked guardedly. 'I shan't have to kiss babies, shall I?'

'Of course you won't, you abysmal chump.'

'I've always heard that kissing babies entered largely into these things.'

'Yes, but it's the candidate who does it, poor blighter. All you have to do is go from house to house urging the inmates to vote for Ginger.'

'Then rely on me. Such an assignment should be well within my scope. Old Ginger!' I said, feeling emotional. 'It will warm the what-d'you-call-its of my heart to see him again.'

'Well, you'll have the opportunity of hotting them up this very afternoon. He's gone to London for the day and wants you to lunch with him.'

'Does he, egad! That's fine. What time?'

'One-thirty.'

'At what spot?'

'Barribault's grill-room.'

'I'll be there. Jeeves,' I said, hanging up, 'You remember Ginger Winship, who used to play Damon to my Pythias?'

'Yes, indeed, sir.'

'They've got an election on at Market Snodsbury, and he's standing in the Conservative interest.'

'So I understood Madam to say, sir.'

'Oh, you caught her remarks?'

'With little or no difficulty, sir. Madam has a penetrating voice.'

'It does penetrate, doesn't it,' I said, massaging the ear

I had been holding to the receiver. 'Good lung power.'

'Extremely, sir.'

'I wonder whether she ever sang lullabies to me in my cradle. If so, it must have scared me cross-eyed, giving me the illusion that the boiler had exploded. However, that is not germane to the issue, which is that we leave for her abode this afternoon. I shall be lunching with Ginger. In my absence, pack a few socks and toothbrushes, will you.'

'Very good, sir,' he replied, and we did not return to the subject of the club book.

3

It was with no little gusto and animation that some hours later I set out for the tryst. This Ginger was one of my oldest buddies, not quite so old as Kipper Herring or Catsmeat Potter-Pirbright, with whom I had plucked the gowans fine at prep school, public school and University, but definitely ancient. Our rooms at Oxford had been adjacent, and it would not be too much to say that from the moment he looked in to borrow a syphon of soda water we became more like brothers than anything, and this state of things had continued after we had both left the seat of learning.

For quite a while he had been a prominent member of the Drones Club, widely known for his effervescence and vivacity, but all of a sudden he had tendered his resignation and gone to live in the country, oddly enough at Steeple Bumpleigh in Essex, where my Aunt Agatha has her lair. This, somebody told me, was due to the circumstance that he had got engaged to a girl of strong character who disapproved of the Drones Club. You get girls like that every now and then, and in my opinion they are best avoided.

Well, naturally this had parted us. He never came to London, and I of course never went to Steeple Bumpleigh. You don't catch me going anywhere near Aunt Agatha unless I have to. No sense in sticking one's neck out. But I had missed him sorely. Oh for the touch of a vanished hand, is how you might put it.

Arriving at Barribault's, I found him in the lobby where you have the pre-luncheon gargle before proceeding to the grill-room, and after the initial

What-ho-ing and What-a-time-since-we-met-ing
inevitable when two vanished hands who haven't seen
each other for ages re-establish contact, he asked me if I
would like one for the tonsils.

'I won't join you,' he said. 'I'm not actually on the
waggon, I have a little light wine at dinner now and
then, but my fiancée wants me to stay off cocktails. She
says they harden the arteries.'

If you are about to ask me if this didn't make me
purse the lips a bit, I can assure you that it did. It
seemed to point to his having gone and got hitched up
with a popsy totally lacking in the proper spirit, and it
bore out what I had been told about her being a girl of
strong character. No one who wasn't could have dashed
the cup from his lips in this manner. She had apparently
made him like it, too, for he had spoken of her not with
the sullen bitterness of one crushed beneath the iron
heel but with devotion in every syllable. Plainly he had
got it up his nose and didn't object to being bossed.

How different from me, I reflected, that time when I
was engaged to my Uncle Percy's bossy daughter
Florence Craye. It didn't last long, because she gave me
the heave-ho and got betrothed to a fellow called
Gorringe who wrote *vers libre*, but while it lasted I felt
like one of those Ethiopian slaves Cleopatra used to
push around, and I chafed more than somewhat.
Whereas Ginger obviously hadn't even started to chafe.
It isn't difficult to spot when a fellow's chafing, and I
could detect none of the symptoms. He seemed to think
that putting the presidential veto on cocktails showed
what an angel of mercy the girl was, always working
with his good at heart.

The Woosters do not like drinking alone, particularly
with a critical eye watching them to see if their arteries
are hardening, so I declined the proffered snort –
reluctantly, for I was athirst – and came straight to the
main item on the agenda paper. On my way to

Barribault's I had, as you may suppose, pondered deeply on this business of him standing for Parliament, and I wanted to know the motives behind the move. It looked cock-eyed to me.

'Aunt Dahlia tells me you are staying with her in order to be handy to Market Snodsbury while giving the electors there the old oil,' I said.

'Yes, she very decently invited me. She was at school with my mother.'

'So she told me. I wonder if her face was as red in those days. How do you like it there?'

'It's a wonderful place.'

'Grade A. Gravel soil, main drainage, spreading grounds and Company's own water. And, of course, Anatole's cooking.'

'Ah!' he said, and I think he would have bared his head, only he hadn't a hat on. 'Very gifted, that man.'

'A wizard,' I agreed. 'His dinners must fortify you for the tasks you have to face. How's the election coming along?'

'All right.'

'Kissed any babies lately?'

'Ah!' he said again, this time with a shudder. I could see that I had touched an exposed nerve. 'What blighters babies are, Bertie, dribbling, as they do, at the side of the mouth. Still, it has to be done. My agent tells me to leave no stone unturned if I want to win the election.'

'But why do you want to win the election? I'd have thought you wouldn't have touched Parliament with a ten-foot pole,' I said, for I knew the society there was very mixed. 'What made you commit this rash act?'

'My fiancée wanted me to,' he said, and as his lips framed the word 'fiancée' his voice took on a sort of tremolo like that of a male turtle dove cooing to a female turtle dove. 'She thought I ought to be carving out a career for myself.'

'Do you want a career?'

'Not much, but she insisted.'

The uneasiness I had felt when he told me the beasel had made him knock off cocktails deepened. His every utterance rendered it more apparent to an experienced man like myself that he had run up against something too hot to handle, and for a moment I thought of advising him to send her a telegram saying it was all off and, this done, to pack a suitcase and catch the next boat to Australia. But feeling that this might give offence I merely asked him what the procedure was when you stood for Parliament – or ran for it, as they would say in America. Not that I particularly wanted to know, but it was something to talk about other than his frightful fiancée.

A cloud passed over his face, which I ought to have mentioned earlier was well worth looking at, the eyes clear, the cheeks tanned, the chin firm, the hair ginger and the nose shapely. It topped off, moreover, a body which also repaid inspection, being muscular and well knit. His general aspect, as a matter of fact, was rather like that presented by Esmond Haddock, the squire of Deverill Hall, where Jeeves's Uncle Charlie Silversmith drew his monthly envelope. He had the same poetic look, as if at any moment about to rhyme June with moon, yet gave the impression, as Esmond did, of being able, if he cared to, to fell an ox with a single blow. I don't know if he had ever actually done this, for one so seldom meets an ox, but in his undergraduate days he had felled people right and left, having represented the University in the ring as a heavyweight a matter of three years. He may have included oxen among his victims.

'You go through hell,' he said, the map still clouded as he recalled the past. 'I had to sit in a room where you could hardly breathe because it was as crowded as the Black Hole of Calcutta and listen to addresses of welcome till midnight. After that I went about making speeches.'

'Well, why aren't you down there, making speeches, now? Have they given you a day off?'

'I came up to get a secretary.'

'Surely you didn't go there without one?'

'No, I had one all right, but my fiancée fired her. They had some sort of disagreement.'

I had pursed the lips a goodish bit when he had told me about his fiancée and the cocktails, and I pursed them to an even greater extent now. The more I heard of this girl he had got engaged to, the less I liked the sound of her. I was thinking how well she would get on with Florence Craye if they happened to meet. Twin souls, I mean to say, each what a housemaid I used to know would have called an overbearing dishpot.

I didn't say so, of course. There is a time to call someone an overbearing dishpot, and a time not to. Criticism of the girl he loved might be taken in ill part, as the expression is, and you don't want an ex-Oxford boxing Blue taking things in ill part with you.

'Have you anyone in mind?' I asked. 'Or are you just going to a secretary bin, accepting what they have in stock?'

'I'm hoping to get hold of an American girl I saw something of before I left London. I was sharing a flat with Boko Fittleworth when he was writing a novel, and she came every day and worked with him. Boko dictates his stuff, and he said she was tops as a shorthand typist. I have her address, but I don't know if she's still there. I'm going round there after lunch. Her name's Magnolia Glendennon.'

'It can't be.'

'Why not?'

'Nobody could have a name like Magnolia.'

'They could if they came from South Carolina, as she did. In the southern states of America you can't throw a brick without hitting a Magnolia. But I was telling you about this business of standing for Parliament. First, of course, you have to get the nomination.'

'How did you manage that?'

'My fiancée fixed it. She knows one of the Cabinet ministers, and he pulled strings. A man named Filmer.'

'Not A. B. Filmer?'

'That's right. Is he a friend of yours?'

'I wouldn't say exactly a friend. I came to know him slightly owing to being chased with him on to the roof of a sort of summer-house by an angry swan. This drew us rather close together for the moment, but we never became really chummy.'

'Where was this?'

'On an island on the lake at my Aunt Agatha's place at Steeple Bumpleigh. Living at Steeple Bumpleigh, you've probably been there.'

He looked at me with a wild surmise, much as those soldiers Jeeves has told me about looked on each other when on a peak in Darien, wherever that is.

'Is Lady Worpledon your aunt?'

'And how.'

'She's never mentioned it.'

'She wouldn't. Her impulse would be to hush it up.'

'Then, good Lord, she must be your cousin.'

'No, my aunt. You can't be both.'

'I mean Florence. Florence Craye, my fiancée.'

It was a shock, I don't mind telling you, and if I hadn't been seated I would probably have reeled. Though I ought not to have been so surprised. Florence was one of those girls who are always getting engaged to someone, first teaming up with Stilton Cheesewright, then me, and finally Percy Gorringe, who was dramatizing her novel *Spindrift*. The play, by the way, had recently been presented to the public at the Duke of York's theatre and had laid an instantaneous egg, coming off on the following Saturday. One of the critics said he had perhaps seen it at a disadvantage because when he saw it the curtain was up. I had wondered a good deal what effect this had had on Florence's haughty spirit.

'You're engaged to Florence?' I yipped, looking at him with a wild surmise.

'Yes. Didn't you know?'

'Nobody tells me anything. Engaged to Florence, eh? Well, well.'

A less tactful man than Bertram Wooster might have gone on to add 'Oh, tough luck!' or something along those lines, for there was no question but that the unhappy man was properly up against it, but if there's one thing the Woosters have in heaping measure, it is tact. I merely gripped his hand, gave it a shake and wished him happiness. He thanked me for this.

'You're lucky,' I said, wearing the mask.

'Don't I know it!'

'She's a charming girl,' I said, still wearing as above.

'That just describes her.'

'Intellectual, too.'

'Distinctly. Writes novels.'

'Always at it.'

'Did you read *Spindrift*?'

'Couldn't put it down,' I said, cunningly not revealing that I hadn't been able to take it up. 'Did you see the play?'

'Twice. Too bad it didn't run. Gorringe's adaptation was the work of an ass.'

'I spotted him as an ass the first time I saw him.'

'It's a pity Florence didn't.'

'Yes. By the way, what became of Gorringe? When last heard of, she was engaged to him.'

'She broke it off.'

'Very wise of her. He had long side-whiskers.'

'She considered him responsible for the failure of the play and told him so.'

'She would.'

'What do you mean she would?'

'Her nature is so frank, honest and forthright.'

'It is, isn't it.'

'She speaks her mind.'

'Invariably.'

'It's an admirable trait.'

'Oh, most.'

'You can't get away with much with a girl like Florence.'

'No.'

We fell into a silence. He was twiddling his fingers and a sort of what-d'you-call-it had come into his manner, as if he wanted to say something but was having trouble in getting it out. I remembered encountering a similar diffidence in the Rev. Stinker Pinker when he was trying to nerve himself to ask me to come to Totleigh Towers, and you find the same thing in dogs when they put a paw on your knee and look up into your face but don't utter, though making it clear that there is a subject on which they are anxious to touch.

'Bertie,' he said at length.

'Hullo?'

'Bertie.'

'Yes?'

'Bertie.'

'Still here. Excuse me asking, but have you any cracked gramophone record blood in you? Perhaps your mother was frightened by one?'

And then it all came out in a rush as if a cork had been pulled.

'Bertie, there's something I must tell you about Florence, though you probably know it already, being a cousin of hers. She's a wonderful girl and practically perfect in every respect, but she has one characteristic which makes it awkward for those who love her and are engaged to her. Don't think I'm criticizing her.'

'No, no.'

'I'm just mentioning it.'

'Exactly.'

'Well, she has no use for a loser. To keep her esteem you have to be a winner. She's like one of those princesses in the fairy tales who set fellows some task to perform, as it might be scaling a mountain of glass or bringing her a hair from the beard of the Great Cham of Tartary, and gave them the brush-off when they couldn't make the grade.'

I recalled the princesses of whom he spoke, and I had always thought them rather fatheads. I mean to say, what sort of foundation for a happy marriage is the bridegroom's ability to scale mountains of glass? A fellow probably wouldn't be called on to do it more than about once every ten years, if that.

'Gorringe,' said Ginger, continuing, 'was a loser, and that dished him. And long ago, someone told me, she was engaged to a gentleman jockey and she chucked him because he took a spill at the canal turn in the Grand National. She's a perfectionist. I admire her for it, of course.'

'Of course.'

'A girl like her is entitled to have high standards.'

'Quite.'

'But, as I say, it makes it awkward for me. She has set her heart on my winning this Market Snodsbury election, heaven knows why, for I never thought she had any interest in politics, and if I lose it, I shall lose her, too. So . . .'

'Now is the time for all good men to come to the aid of the party?'

'Exactly. You are going to canvass for me. Well, canvass like a ton of bricks, and see that Jeeves does the same. I've simply got to win.'

'You can rely on us.'

'Thank you, Bertie, I knew I could. And now let's go in and have a bite of lunch.'

4

Having restored the tissues with the excellent nourishment which Barribault's hotel always provides and arranged that Ginger was to pick me up in his car later in the afternoon, my own sports model being at the vet's with some nervous ailment, we parted, he to go in search of Magnolia Glendennon, I to walk back to the Wooster GHQ.

It was, as you may suppose, in thoughtful mood that I made my way through London's thoroughfares. I was reading a novel of suspense the other day in which the heroine, having experienced a sock in the eye or two, was said to be lost in a maze of mumbling thoughts, and that description would have fitted me like the paper on the wall.

My heart was heavy. When a man is an old friend and pretty bosom at that, it depresses you to hear that he's engaged to Florence Craye. I recalled my own emotions when I had found myself in that unpleasant position. I had felt like someone trapped in the underground den of the Secret Nine.

Though, mark you, there's nothing to beef about in her outer crust. At the time when she was engaged to Stilton Cheesewright I remember recording in the archives that she was tall and willowy with a terrific profile and luxuriant platinum-blonde hair; the sort of girl who might, as far as looks were concerned, have been the star unit of the harem of one of the better-class Sultans; and though I hadn't seen her for quite a while, I presumed that these conditions still prevailed. The fact that Ginger, when speaking of her, had gone so readily into his turtle dove impersonation seemed to indicate as much.

Looks, however, aren't everything. Against this pin-up-ness of hers you had to put the bossiness which would lead her to expect the bloke she married to behave like a Hollywood Yes-man. From childhood up she had been . . . I can't think of the word . . . begins with an i . . . No, it's gone . . . but I can give you the idea. When at my private school I once won a prize for Scripture Knowledge, which naturally involved a lot of researching into Holy Writ, and in the course of my researches I came upon the story of the military chap who used to say 'Come' and they cometh and 'Go' and they goeth. I have always thought that that was Florence in a nutshell. She would have given short shrift, as the expression is, to anyone who had gone when she said 'Come' or the other way round. Imperious, that's the word I was groping for. She was as imperious as a traffic cop. Little wonder that the heart was heavy. I felt that Ginger, mistaking it for a peach, had plucked a lemon in the garden of love.

And then my meditations took a less sombre turn. This often happens after a good lunch, even if you haven't had a cocktail. I reminded myself that many married men positively enjoy being kept on their toes by the little woman, and possibly Ginger might be one of them. He might take the view that when the little w made him sit up and beg and snap lumps of sugar off his nose, it was a compliment really, because it showed that she was taking an interest.

Feeling a bit more cheerful, I reached for my cigarette case and was just going to open it, when like an ass I dropped it and it fell into the road. And as I stepped from the pavement to retrieve it there was a sudden tooting in my rear, and whirling on my axis I perceived that in about another two ticks I was going to be rammed amidships by a taxi.

The trouble about whirling on your axis, in case you didn't know, is that you're liable, if not an adagio dancer, to trip over your feet, and this was what I proceeded to do. My left shoe got all mixed up with my right ankle, I tottered, swayed, and after a brief pause came down like some noble tree beneath the woodman's axe, and I was sitting there lost in a maze of numbing thoughts, when an unseen hand attached itself to my arm and jerked me back to safety. The taxi went on and turned the corner.

Well, of course the first thing the man of sensibility does on these occasions is to thank his brave preserver. I turned to do this, and blow me tight if the b.p. wasn't Jeeves. Came as a complete surprise. I couldn't think what he was doing there, and for an instant the idea occurred to me that this might be his astral body.

'Jeeves!' I ejaculated. I'm pretty sure that's the word. Anyway, I'll risk it.

'Good afternoon, sir. I trust you are not too discommoded. That was a somewhat narrow squeak.'

'It was indeed. I don't say my whole life passed before me, but a considerable chunk of it did. But for you –'

'Not at all, sir.'

'Yes, you and you only saved me from appearing in tomorrow's obituary column.'

'A pleasure, sir.'

'It's amazing how you always turn up at the crucial moment, like the United States Marines. I remember how you did when A. B. Filmer and I were having our altercation with that swan, and there were other occasions too numerous to mention. Well, you will certainly get a rave notice in my prayers next time I make them. But how do you happen to be in these parts? Where are we, by the way?'

'This is Curzon Street, sir.'

'Of course. I'd have known that if I hadn't been musing.'

'You were musing, sir?'

'Deeply. I'll tell you about it later. This is where your club is, isn't it?'

'Yes, sir, just round the corner. In your absence and having completed the packing, I decided to lunch there.'

'Thank heaven you did. If you hadn't, I'd have been . . . what's that gag of yours? Something about wheels.'

'Less than the dust beneath thy chariot wheels, sir.'

'Or, rather, the cabby's chariot wheels. Why are you looking at me with such a searching eye, Jeeves?'

'I was thinking that your misadventure had left you somewhat dishevelled, sir. If I might suggest it, I think we should repair to the Junior Ganymede now.'

'I see what you mean. You would give me a wash and brush-up?'

'Just so, sir.'

'And perhaps a whisky-and-soda?'

'Certainly, sir.'

'I need one sorely. Ginger's practically on the waggon, so there were no cocktails before lunch. And do you know why he's practically on the waggon? Because the girl he's engaged to has made him take that foolish step. And do you know who the girl he's engaged to is? My cousin Florence Craye.'

'Indeed, sir?'

Well, I hadn't expected him to roll his eyes and leap about, because he never does no matter how sensational the news item, but I could see by the way one of his eyebrows twitched and rose perhaps an eighth of an inch that I had interested him. And there was what is called a wealth of meaning in that 'Indeed, sir?' He was conveying his opinion that this was a bit of luck for Bertram, because a girl you have once been engaged to is always a lurking menace till she gets engaged to someone else and so cannot decide at any moment to play a return date. I got the message and thoroughly agreed with him, though naturally I didn't say so.

Jeeves, you see, is always getting me out of entanglements with the opposite sex, and he knows all about the various females who from time to time have come within an ace of hauling me to the altar rails, but of course we don't discuss them. To do so, we feel, would come under the head of bandying a woman's name, and the Woosters do not bandy women's names. Nor do the Jeeveses. I can't speak for his Uncle Charlie Silversmith, but I should imagine that he, too, has his code of ethics in this respect. These things generally run in families.

So I merely filled him in about her making Ginger stand for Parliament and the canvassing we were going to undertake, urging him to do his utmost to make the electors think along the right lines, and he said 'Yes, sir' and 'Very good, sir' and 'I quite understand, sir', and we proceeded to the Junior Ganymede.

An extremely cosy club it proved to be. I didn't wonder that he liked to spend so much of his leisure there. It lacked the sprightliness of the Drones. I shouldn't think there was much bread and sugar thrown about at lunch time, and you would hardly expect that there would be when you reflected that the membership consisted of elderly butlers and gentlemen's gentlemen of fairly ripe years, but as regards comfort it couldn't be faulted. The purler I had taken had left me rather tender in the fleshy parts, and it was a relief after I had been washed and brushed up and was on the spruce side once more to sink into a well-stuffed chair in the smoking-room.

Sipping my whisky-and-s., I brought the conversation round again to Ginger and his election, which was naturally the front page stuff of the day.

'Do you think he has a chance, Jeeves?'

He weighed the question for a moment, as if dubious as to where he would place his money.

'It is difficult to say, sir. Market Snodsbury, like so

many English country towns, might be described as straitlaced. It sets a high value on respectability.'

'Well, Ginger's respectable enough.'

'True, sir, but, as you are aware, he has had a Past.'

'Not much of one.'

'Sufficient, however, to prejudice the voters, should they learn of it.'

'Which they can't possibly do. I suppose he's in the club book –'

'Eleven pages, sir.'

' – But you assure me that the contents of the club book will never be revealed.'

'Never, sir. Mr Winship has nothing to fear from that quarter.'

His words made me breathe more freely.

'Jeeves,' I said, 'your words make me breathe more freely. As you know, I am always a bit uneasy about the club book. Kept under lock and key, is it?'

'Not actually under lock and key, sir, but it is safely bestowed in the secretary's office.'

'Then there's nothing to worry about.'

'I would not say that, sir. Mr Winship must have had companions in his escapades, and they might inadvertently make some reference to them which would get into gossip columns in the Press and thence into the Market Snodsbury journals. I believe there are two of these, one rigidly opposed to the Conservative interest which Mr Winship is representing. It is always a possibility, and the results would be disastrous. I have no means at the moment of knowing the identity of Mr Winship's opponent, but he is sure to be a model of respectability whose past can bear the strictest investigation.'

'You're pretty gloomy, Jeeves. Why aren't you gathering rosebuds? The poet Herrick would shake his head.'

'I am sorry, sir. I did not know that you were taking

Mr Winship's fortunes so much to heart, or I would have been more guarded in my speech. Is victory in the election of such importance to him?'

'It's vital. Florence will hand him his hat if he doesn't win.'

'Surely not, sir?'

'That's what he says, and I think he's right. His observations on the subject were most convincing. He says she's a perfectionist and has no use for a loser. It is well established that she handed Percy Gorringe the pink slip because the play he made of her novel only ran three nights.'

'Indeed, sir?'

'Well-documented fact.'

'Then let us hope that what I fear will not happen, sir.'

We were sitting there hoping that what he feared would not happen, when a shadow fell on my whisky-and-s. and I saw that we had been joined by another member of the Junior Ganymede, a smallish, plumpish, Gawd-help-us-ish member wearing clothes more suitable for the country than the town and a tie that suggested that he belonged to the Brigade of Guards, though I doubted if this was the case. As to his manner, I couldn't get a better word for it at the moment than 'familiar', but I looked it up later in Jeeves's *Dictionary of Synonyms* and found that it had been unduly intimate, too free, forward, lacking in proper reserve, deficient in due respect, impudent, bold and intrusive. Well, when I tell you that the first thing he did was to prod Jeeves in the lower ribs with an uncouth forefinger, you will get the idea.

'Hullo, Reggie,' he said, and I froze in my chair, stunned by the revelation that Jeeves's first name was Reginald. It had never occurred to me before that he had a first name. I couldn't help thinking what embarrassment would have been caused if it had been Bertie.

'Good afternoon,' said Jeeves, and I could see that the chap was not one of his inner circle of friends. His voice was cold, and anyone less lacking in proper reserve and deficient in due respect would have spotted this and recoiled.

The Gawd-help-us fellow appeared to notice nothing amiss. His manner continued to be that of one who has met a pal of long standing.

'How's yourself, Reggie?'

'I am in tolerably good health, thank you.'

'Lost weight, haven't you? You ought to live in the country like me and get good country butter.' He turned to me. 'And you ought to be more careful, cocky, dancing about in the middle of the street like that. I was in that cab and I thought you were a goner. You're Wooster, aren't you?'

'Yes,' I said, amazed. I hadn't known I was such a public figure.

'Thought so. I don't often forget a face. Well, I can't stay chatting with you. I've got to see the secretary about something. Nice to have seen you, Reggie.'

'Goodbye.'

'Nice to have seen you, Wooster, old man.'

I thanked him, and he withdrew. I turned to Jeeves, that wild surmise I was speaking about earlier functioning on all twelve cylinders.

'Who was that?'

He did not reply immediately, plainly too ruffled for speech. He had to take a sip of his liqueur brandy before he was master of himself. His manner, when he did speak, was that of one who would have preferred to let the whole thing drop.

'The person you mentioned at the breakfast table, sir. Bingley,' he said, pronouncing the name as if it soiled his lips.

I was astounded. You could have knocked me down with a toothpick.

'Bingley? I'd never have recognized him. He's changed completely. He was quite thin when I knew him, and very gloomy, you might say sinister. Always seemed to be brooding silently on the coming revolution, when he would be at liberty to chase me down Park Lane with a dripping knife.'

The brandy seemed to have restored Jeeves. He spoke now with his customary calm.

'I believe his political views were very far to the left at the time when he was in your employment. They changed when he became a man of property.'

'A man of property, is he?'

'An uncle of his in the grocery business died and left him a house and a comfortable sum of money.'

'I suppose it often happens that the views of fellows like Bingley change when they come into money.'

'Very frequently. They regard the coming revolution from a different standpoint.'

'I see what you mean. They don't want to be chased down Park Lane with dripping knives themselves. Is he still a gentleman's gentleman?'

'He has retired. He lives a life of leisure in Market Snodsbury.'

'Market Snodsbury? That's funny.'

'Sir?'

'Odd, I mean, that he should live in Market Snodsbury.'

'Many people do, sir.'

'But when that's just where we're going. Sort of a coincidence. His uncle's house is there, I suppose.'

'One presumes so.'

'We may be seeing something of him.'

'I hope not, sir. I disapprove of Bingley. He is dishonest. Not a man to be trusted.'

'What makes you think so?'

'It is merely a feeling.'

Well, it was no skin off my nose. A busy man like

myself hasn't time to go about trusting Bingley. All I demanded of Bingley was that if our paths should cross he would remain sober and keep away from carving knives. Live and let live is the Wooster motto. I finished my whisky-and-soda and rose.

'Well,' I said, 'there's one thing. Holding the strong Conservative views he does, it ought to be a snip to get him to vote for Ginger. And now we'd better be getting along. Ginger is driving us down in his car, and I don't know when he'll be coming to fetch us. Thanks for your princely hospitality, Jeeves. You have brought new life to the exhausted frame.'

'Not at all, sir.'

5

Ginger turned up in due course, and on going out to the
car I saw that he had managed to get hold of Magnolia
all right, for there was a girl sitting in the back and when
he introduced us his 'Mr Wooster, Miss Glendennon'
told the story.

Nice girl she seemed to me and quite nice-looking. I
wouldn't say hers was the face that launched a thousand
ships, to quote one of Jeeves's gags, and this was
probably all to the good, for Florence, I imagine, would
have had a word to say if Ginger had returned from his
travels with something in tow calculated to bring a
whistle to the lips of all beholders. A man in his position
has to exercise considerable care in his choice of
secretaries, ruling out anything that might have done
well in the latest Miss America contest. But you could
certainly describe her appearance as pleasant. She gave
me the impression of being one of those quiet,
sympathetic girls whom you could tell your troubles to
in the certain confidence of having your hand held and
your head patted. The sort of girl you could go to and say
'I say, I've just committed a murder and it's worrying me
rather,' and she would reply, 'There, there, try not to
think about it, it's the sort of thing that might happen to
anybody.' The little mother, in short, with the added
attraction of being tops at shorthand and typing. I could
have wished Ginger's affairs in no better hands.

Jeeves brought out the suitcases and stowed them
away, and Ginger asked me to do the driving, as he had a
lot of business to go into with his new secretary, giving
her the low-down on her duties, I suppose. We set out,

accordingly, with me and Jeeves in front, and about the journey down there is nothing of interest to report. I was in merry mood throughout, as always when about to get another whack at Anatole's cooking. Jeeves presumably felt the same, for he, like me, is one of that master skillet-wielder's warmest admirers, but whereas I sang a good deal as we buzzed along, he maintained, as is his custom, the silent reserve of a stuffed frog, never joining in the chorus, though cordially invited to.

Arriving at journey's end, we all separated. Jeeves attended to the luggage, Ginger took Magnolia Glendennon off to his office, and I made my way to the drawing-room, which I found empty. There seemed to be nobody about, as so often happens when you fetch up at a country house lateish in the afternoon. No sign of Aunt Dahlia, nor of Uncle Tom, her mate. I toyed with the idea of going to see if the latter was in the room where he keeps his collection of old silver, but thought better not. Uncle Tom is one of those enthusiastic collectors who, if in a position to grab you, detain you for hours, talking about sconces, foliation, ribbon wreaths in high relief and gadroon borders, and one wants as little of that sort of thing as can be managed.

I might have gone to pay my respects to Anatole, but there again I thought better not. He, too, is inclined to the long monologue when he gets you in his power, his pet subject the state of his interior. He suffers from bouts of what he calls *mal au foie*, and his conversation would be of greater interest to a medical man than to a layman like myself. I don't know why it is, but when somebody starts talking to me about his liver I never can listen with real enjoyment.

On the whole, the thing to do seemed to be to go for a saunter in the extensive grounds and messuages.

It was one of those heavy, sultry afternoons when Nature seems to be saying to itself 'Now shall I or shall I not scare the pants off these people with a hell of a thunderstorm?', but I decided to risk it. There's a small wooded bit not far from the house which I've always been fond of, and thither I pushed along. This wooded bit contains one or two rustic benches for the convenience of those who wish to sit and meditate, and as I hove alongside the first of these I saw that there was an expensive-looking camera on it.

It surprised me somewhat, for I had no idea that Aunt Dahlia had taken to photography, but of course you never know what aunts will be up to next. The thought that occurred to me almost immediately was that if there was going to be a thunderstorm, it would be accompanied by rain, and rain falling on a camera doesn't do it any good. I picked the thing up, accordingly, and started off with it to take it back to the house, feeling that the old relative would thank me for my thoughtfulness, possibly with tears in her eyes, when there was a sudden bellow and an individual emerged from behind a clump of bushes. Startled me considerably, I don't mind telling you.

He was an extremely stout individual with a large pink face and a Panama hat with a pink ribbon. A perfect stranger to me, and I wondered what he was doing here. He didn't look the sort of crony Aunt Dahlia would have invited to stay, and still less Uncle Tom, who is so allergic to guests that when warned of their approach he generally makes a bolt for it and disappears, leaving not a wrack behind as I have heard Jeeves put it. However, as I was saying, you never know what aunts will be up to next and no doubt the ancestor had had some good reason for asking the chap to come and mix, so I beamed civilly and opened the conversation with a genial 'Hullo there'.

'Nice day,' I said, continuing to beam civilly. 'Or, rather, not so frightfully nice. Looks as if we were in for a thunderstorm.'

Something seemed to have annoyed him. The pink of

his face had deepened to about the colour of his Panama hat ribbon, and both his chins trembled slightly.

'Damn thunderstorms!' he responded – curtly, I suppose, would be the word – and I said I didn't like them myself. It was the lightning, I added, that I chiefly objected to.

'They say it never strikes twice in the same place, but then it hasn't got to.'

'Damn the lightning! What are you doing with my camera?'

This naturally opened up a new line of thought.

'Oh, is this your camera?'

'Yes, it is.'

'I was taking it to the house.'

'You were, were you?'

'I didn't want it to get wet.'

'Oh? And who are you?'

I was glad he had asked me that. His whole manner had made it plain to a keen mind like mine that he was under the impression that he had caught me in the act of absconding with his property, and I was glad to have the opportunity of presenting my credentials. I could see that if we were ever to have a good laugh together over this amusing misunderstanding, there would have to be a certain amount of preliminary spadework.

'Wooster is the name,' I said. 'I'm my aunt's nephew. I mean,' I went on, for those last words seemed to me not to have rung quite right, 'Mrs Travers is my aunt.'

'You are staying in the house?'

'Yes. Just arrived.'

'Oh?' he said again, but this time in what you might call a less hostile tone.

'Yes,' I said, rubbing it in.

There followed a silence, presumably occupied by him in turning things over in his mind in the light of my statement and examining them in depth and then he said 'Oh?' once more and stumped off.

I made no move to accompany him. What little I had had of his society had been ample. As we were staying in the same house, we would no doubt meet occasionally, but not, I resolved, if I saw him first. The whole episode reminded me of my first encounter with Sir Watkyn Bassett and the misunderstanding about his umbrella. That had left me shaken, and so had this. I was glad to have a rustic bench handy, so that I could sit and try to bring my nervous system back into shape. The sky had become more and more inky I suppose is the word I want and the odds on a thunderstorm shorter than ever, but I still lingered. It was only when there came from above a noise like fifty-seven trucks going over a wooden bridge that I felt that an immediate move would be judicious. I rose and soon gathered speed, and I had reached the French window of the drawing-room and was on the point of popping through, when from within there came the sound of a human voice. On second thoughts delete the word 'human', for it was the voice of my recent acquaintance with whom I had chatted about cameras.

I halted. There was a song I used to sing in my bath at one time, the refrain or burthen of which began with the words 'I stopped and I looked and I listened', and this was what I did now, except for the looking. It wasn't raining, nor was there any repetition of the trucks-going-over-a-wooden-bridge noise. It was as though Nature had said to itself 'Oh to hell with it' and decided that it was too much trouble to have a thunderstorm after all. So I wasn't getting struck by lightning or even wet, which enabled me to remain in status quo.

The camera bloke was speaking to some unseen companion, and what he said was;

'Wooster, his name is. Says he's Mrs Travers's nephew.'

It was plain that I had arrived in the middle of a

conversation. The words must have been preceded by a
query, possibly 'Oh, by the way, do you happen to know
who a tall, slender, good-looking – I might almost say
fascinating – young man I was talking to outside there
would be?', though of course possibly not. That, at any
rate, must have been the gist, and I suppose the party of
the second part had replied 'No, sorry, I can't place him',
or words to that effect. Whereupon the camera chap had
spoken as above. And as he spoke as above a snort rang
through the quiet room; a voice, speaking with every
evidence of horror and disgust, exclaimed 'Wooster!';
and I quivered from hair-do to shoe sole. I may even
have gasped, but fortunately not loud enough to be
audible beyond the French window.

For it was the voice of Lord Sidcup – or, as I shall
always think of him, no matter how many titles he may
have inherited, Spode. Spode, mark you, whom I had
thought and hoped I had seen the last of after dusting the
dust of Totleigh Towers from the Wooster feet; Spode,
who went about seeking whom he might devour and
from early boyhood had been a hissing and a by-word to
all right-thinking men. Little wonder that for a moment
everything seemed to go black and I had to clutch at a
passing rose bush to keep from falling.

This Spode, I must explain for the benefit of the
newcomers who have not read the earlier chapters of my
memoirs, was a character whose path had crossed mine
many a time and oft, as the expression is, and always
with the most disturbing results. I have spoken of the
improbability of a beautiful friendship ever getting under
way between me and the camera chap, but the
likelihood of any such fusion of souls, as I have heard
Jeeves call it, between me and Spode was even more
remote. Our views on each other were definite. His was
that what England needed if it was to become a land fit
for heroes to live in was fewer and better Woosters,
while I had always felt that there was nothing wrong

with England that a ton of bricks falling from a height on Spode's head wouldn't cure.

'You know him?' said the camera chap.

'I'm sorry to say I do,' said Spode, speaking like Sherlock Holmes asked if he knew Professor Moriarty. 'How did you happen to meet him?'

'I found him making off with my camera.'

'Ha!'

'Naturally I thought he was stealing it. But if he's really Mrs Travers's nephew, I suppose I was mistaken.'

Spode would have none of this reasoning, though it seemed pretty sound to me. He snorted again with even more follow-through than the first time.

'Being Mrs Travers's nephew means nothing. If he was the nephew of an archbishop he would behave in a precisely similar manner. Wooster would steal anything that was not nailed down, provided he could do it unobserved. He couldn't have known you were there?'

'No. I was behind a bush.'

'And your camera looks a good one.'

'Cost me a lot of money.'

'Then of course he was intending to steal it. He must have thought he had dropped into a bit of good luck. Let me tell you about Wooster. The first time I met him was in an antique shop. I had gone there with Sir Watkyn Bassett, my future father-in-law. He collects old silver. And Sir Watkyn had propped his umbrella up against a piece of furniture. Wooster was there, but lurking, so we didn't see him.'

'In a dark corner, perhaps?'

'Or behind something. The first we saw of him, he was sneaking off with Sir Watkyn's umbrella.'

'Pretty cool.'

'Oh, he's cool all right. These fellows have to be.'

'I suppose so. Must take a nerve of ice.'

To say that I boiled with justifiable indignation would not be putting it too strongly. As I have recorded elsewhere, there was a ready explanation of my behaviour. I had come out without my umbrella that morning, and, completely forgetting that I had done so, I had grasped old Bassett's, obeying the primeval instinct which makes a man without an umbrella reach out for the nearest one in sight, like a flower groping towards the sun. Unconsciously, as it were.

Spode resumed. They had taken a moment off, no doubt in order to brood on my delinquency. His voice now was that of one about to come to the high spot in his narrative.

'You'll hardly believe this, but soon after that he turned up at Totleigh Towers, Sir Watkyn's house in Gloucestershire.'

'Incredible!'

'I thought you'd think so.'

'Disguised, of course? A wig? A false beard? His cheeks stained with walnut juice?'

'No, he came quite openly, invited by my future wife. She has a sort of sentimental pity for him. I think she hopes to reform him.'

'Girls will be girls.'

'Yes, but I wish they wouldn't.'

'Did you rebuke your future wife?'

'I wasn't in a position to then.'

'Probably a wise thing, anyway. I once rebuked the girl I wanted to marry, and she went off and teamed up with a stockbroker. So what happened?'

'He stole a valuable piece of silver. A sort of silver cream jug. A cow-creamer, they call it.'

'My doctor forbids me cream. You had him arrested, of course?'

'We couldn't. No evidence.'

'But you knew he had done it?'

'We were certain.'

'Well, that's how it goes. See any more of him after that?'

'This you will *not* believe. He came to Totleigh Towers *again*!'

'Impossible!'

'Once more invited by my future wife.'

'Would that be the Miss Bassett who arrived last night?'

'Yes, that was Madeline.'

'Lovely girl. I met her in the garden before breakfast. My doctor recommends a breath of fresh air in the early morning. Did you know she thinks those bits of mist you see on the grass are the elves' bridal veils?'

'She has a very whimsical fancy.'

'And nothing to be done about it, I suppose. But you were telling me about this second visit of Wooster's to Totleigh Towers. Did he steal anything this time?'

'An amber statuette worth a thousand pounds.'

'He certainly gets around,' said the camera chap with, I thought, a sort of grudging admiration. 'I hope you had him arrested?'

'We did. He spent the night in the local gaol. But next morning Sir Watkyn weakened and let him off.'

'Mistaken kindness.'

'So I thought.'

The camera chap didn't comment further on this, though he was probably thinking that of all the soppy families introduced to his notice the Bassetts took the biscuit.

'Well, I'm very much obliged to you,' he said, 'for telling me about this man Wooster and putting me on my guard. I've brought a very valuable bit of old silver with me. I am hoping to sell it to Mr Travers. If Wooster learns of this, he is bound to try to purloin it, and I can tell you, that if he does and I catch him, there will be none of this nonsense of a single night in gaol. He will get the stiffest sentence the law can provide. And now, how about a quick game of billiards before dinner? My doctor advises a little gentle exercise.'

'I should enjoy it.'

'Then let us be getting along.'

Having given them time to remove themselves, I went in and sank down on a sofa. I was profoundly stirred, for if you think fellows enjoy listening to the sort of thing Spode had been saying about me, you're wrong. My pulse was rapid and my brow wet with honest sweat, like the village blacksmith's. I was badly in need of alcoholic refreshment, and just as my tongue was beginning to stick out and blacken at the roots, shiver my timbers if Jeeves didn't enter left centre with a tray containing all the makings. St Bernard dogs, you probably know, behave in a similar way in the Alps and are well thought of in consequence.

Mingled with the ecstasy which the sight of him aroused in my bosom was a certain surprise that he should be acting as cup-bearer. It was a job that should rightly have fallen into the province of Seppings, Aunt Dahlia's butler.

'Hullo, Jeeves!' I ejaculated.

'Good evening, sir. I have unpacked your effects. Can I pour you a whisky-and-soda?'

'You can indeed. But what are you doing, buttling? This mystifies me greatly. Where's Seppings?'

'He has retired to bed, sir, with an attack of indigestion consequent upon a too liberal indulgence in Monsieur Anatole's cooking at lunch. I am undertaking his duties for the time being.'

'Very white of you, and very white of you to pop up at this particular moment. I have had a shock, Jeeves.'

'I am sorry to hear that, sir.'

'Did you know Spode was here?'

'Yes, sir.'

'And Miss Bassett?'

'Yes, sir.'

'We might as well be at Totleigh Towers.'

'I can appreciate your dismay, sir, but fellow guests are easily avoided.'

'Yes, and if you avoid them, what do they do? They go about telling men in Panama hats you're a sort of cross between Raffles and one of those fellows who pinch bags at railway stations,' I said, and in a few crisp words I gave him a résumé of Spode's remarks.

'Most disturbing, sir.'

'Very. You know and I know how sound my motives were for everything I did at Totleigh, but what if Spode tells Aunt Agatha?'

'An unlikely contingency, sir.'

'I suppose it is.'

'But I know just how you feel, sir. Who steals my purse steals trash; 'tis something, nothing; 'twas mine, 'tis his, and has been slave to thousands. But he who filches from me my good name robs me of that which not enriches him and makes me poor indeed.'

'Neat, that. Your own?'

'No, sir. Shakespeare's.'

'Shakespeare said some rather good things.'

'I understand that he has given uniform satisfaction, sir. Shall I mix you another?'

'Do just that thing, Jeeves, and with all convenient speed.'

He had completed his St Bernard act and withdrawn, and I was sipping my second rather more slowly than the first, when the door opened and Aunt Dahlia bounded in, all joviality and rosy complexion.

6

I never see this relative without thinking how odd it is that one sister – call her Sister A – can be so unlike another sister, whom we will call Sister B. My Aunt Agatha, for instance, is tall and thin and looks rather like a vulture in the Gobi desert, while Aunt Dahlia is short and solid, like a scrum half in the game of Rugby football. In disposition, too, they differ widely. Aunt Agatha is cold and haughty, though presumably unbending a bit when conducting human sacrifices at the time of the full moon, as she is widely rumoured to do, and her attitude towards me has always been that of an austere governess, causing me to feel as if I were six years old and she had just caught me stealing jam from the jam cupboard; whereas Aunt Dahlia is as jovial and bonhomous as a pantomime dame in a Christmas pantomime. Curious.

I welcomed her with a huge 'Hello', in both syllables of which a nephew's love and esteem could be easily detected, and went so far as to imprint an affectionate kiss on her brow. Later I would take her roundly to task for filling the house with Spodes and Madeline Bassetts and bulging bounders in Panama hats, but that could wait.

She returned my greeting with one of her uncouth hunting cries – 'Yoicks', if I remember correctly. Apparently, when you've been with the Quorn and the Pytchley for some time, you drop into the habit of departing from basic English.

'So here you are, young Bertie.'

'You never spoke a truer word. Up and doing, with a heart for any fate.'

'As thirsty as ever, I observe. I thought I would find you tucking into the drinks.'

'Purely medicinal. I've had a shock.'

'What gave you that?'

'Suddenly becoming apprised of the fact that the blighter Spode was my fellow guest,' I said, feeling that I couldn't have a better cue for getting down to my recriminations. 'What on earth was the idea of inviting a fiend in human shape like that here?' I said, for I knew she shared my opinion of the seventh Earl of Sidcup. 'You have told me many a time and oft that you consider him one of Nature's gravest blunders. And yet you go out of your way to court his society, if court his society is the expression I want. You must have been off your onion, old ancestor.'

It was a severe ticking-off, and you would have expected the blush of shame to have mantled her cheeks, not that you would have noticed it much, her complexion being what it was after all those winters in the hunting field, but she was apparently imp-something, impervious, that's the word, to remorse. She remained what Anatole would have called as cool as some cucumbers.

'Ginger asked me to. He wanted Spode to speak for him at this election. He knows him slightly.'

'Far the best way of knowing Spode.'

'He needs all the help he can get, and Spode's one of those silver-tongued orators you read about. Extraordinary gift of the gab he has. He could get into Parliament without straining a sinew.'

I dare say she was right, but I resented any praise of Spode. I made clear my displeasure by responding curtly:

'Then why doesn't he?'

'He can't, you poor chump. He's a lord.'

'Don't they allow lords in?'

'No, they don't.'

'I see,' I said, rather impressed by this proof that the House of Commons drew the line somewhere. 'Well, I suppose you aren't so much to blame as I had thought. How do you get on with him?'

'I avoid him as much as possible.'

'Very shrewd. I shall do the same. We now come to Madeline Bassett. She's here, too. Why?'

'Oh, Madeline came along for the ride. She wanted to be near Spode. An extraordinary thing to want, I agree. Morbid, you might call it. Florence Craye, of course, has come to help Ginger's campaign.'

I started visibly. In fact, I jumped about six inches, as if a skewer or knitting-needle had come through the seat of my chair.

'You don't mean Florence is here as well?'

'With bells on. You seem perturbed.'

'I'm all of a twitter. It never occurred to me that when I came here I would be getting into a sort of population explosion.'

'Who ever told you about population explosions?'

'Jeeves. They are rather a favourite subject of his. He says if something isn't done pretty soon –'

'I'll bet he said, If steps are not taken shortly through the proper channels.'

'He did, as a matter of fact. He said, If steps aren't taken shortly through the proper channels, half the world will soon be standing on the other half's shoulders.'

'All right if you're one of the top layer.'

'Yes, there's that, of course.'

'Though even then it would be uncomfortable. Tricky sort of balancing act.'

'True.'

'And difficult to go for a stroll if you wanted to stretch the legs. And one wouldn't get much hunting.'

'Not much.'

We mused for awhile on what lay before us, and I remember thinking that present conditions, even with Spode and Madeline and Florence on the premises, suited one better. From this to thinking of Uncle Tom was but a step. It seemed to me that the poor old buster must be on the verge of a nervous breakdown. Even a single guest is sometimes too much for him.

'How,' I asked, 'is Uncle Tom bearing up under this invasion of his cabin?'

She stared incredibly or rather incredulously.

'Did you expect to find him here playing his banjo? My poor halfwitted child, he was off to the south of France the moment he learned that danger threatened. I had a picture postcard from him yesterday. He's having a wonderful time and wishes I was there.'

'And don't you mind all these blighters overrunning the place?'

'I would prefer it if they went elsewhere, but I treat them with saintly forbearance because I feel it's all helping Ginger.'

'How do things look in that direction?'

'An even bet, I would say. The slightest thing might turn the scale. He and his opponent are having a debate in a day or two, and a good deal, you might say everything, depends on that.'

'Who's the opponent?'

'Local talent. A barrister.'

'Jeeves says Market Snodsbury is very straitlaced, and if the electors found out about Ginger's past they would heave him out without even handing him his hat.'

'Has he a past?'

'I wouldn't call it that. Pure routine, I'd describe it as. In the days before he fell under Florence's spell he was rather apt to get slung out of restaurants for throwing eggs at the electric fan, and he seldom escaped unjugged on Boat Race night for pinching policemen's helmets. Would that lose him votes?'

'Lose him votes? If it was brought to Market Snodsbury's attention, I doubt if he would get a single one. That sort of thing might be overlooked in the cities of the plain, but not in Market Snodsbury. So for heaven's sake don't go babbling about it to everyone you meet.'

'My dear old ancestor, am I likely to?'

'Very likely, I should say. You know how fat your head is.'

I would have what-d'you-call-it-ed this slur, and with vehemence, but the adjective she had used reminded me that we had been talking all this time and I hadn't enquired about the camera chap.

'By the way,' I said, 'who would a fat fellow be?'

'Someone fond of starchy foods who had omitted to watch his calories, I imagine. What on earth, if anything, are you talking about?'

I saw that my question had been too abrupt. I hastened to clarify it.

'Strolling in the grounds and messuages just now I encountered an obese bird in a Panama hat with a pink ribbon, and I was wondering who he was and how he came to be staying here. He didn't look the sort of bloke for whom you would be putting out mats with "Welcome" on them. He gave me the impression of being a thug of the first order.'

My words seemed to have touched a chord. Rising nimbly, she went to the door and opened it, then to the French window and looked out, plainly in order to ascertain that nobody – except me, of course – was listening. Spies in spy stories do the same kind of thing when about to make communications which are for your ears only.

'I suppose I'd better tell you about him,' she said.

I intimated that I would be an attentive audience.

'That's L. P. Runkle, and I want you to exercise your charm on him, such as it is. He has to be conciliated and sucked up to.'

'Why, is he someone special?'

'You bet he's someone special. He's a big financier, Runkle's Enterprises. Loaded with money.'

It seemed to me that these words could have but one significance.

'You're hoping to touch him?'

'Such is indeed my aim. But not for myself. I want to get a round sum out of him for Tuppy Glossop.'

Her allusion was to the nephew of Sir Roderick Glossop, the well-known nerve specialist and loony doctor, once a source of horror and concern to Bertram but now one of my leading pals. He calls me Bertie, I call him Roddy. Tuppy, too, is one of my immediate circle of buddies, in spite of the fact that he once betted me I couldn't swing myself from end to end of the swimming bath at the Drones, and when I came to the last ring I found he had looped it back, giving me no option but to drop into the water in faultless evening dress. This had been like a dagger in the bosom for a considerable period, but eventually Time the great healer had ironed things out and I had forgiven him. He has been betrothed to Aunt Dahlia's daughter Angela for ages, and I had never been able to understand why they hadn't got around to letting the wedding bells get cracking. I had been expecting every day for ever so long to be called on to weigh in with the silver fish-slice, but the summons never came.

Naturally I asked if Tuppy was hard up, and she said he wasn't begging his bread and nosing about in the gutters for cigarette ends, but he hadn't enough to marry on.

'Thanks to L. P. Runkle. I'll tell you the whole story.'

'Do.'

'Did you ever meet Tuppy's late father?'

'Once. I remember him as a dreamy old bird of the absent-minded professor type.'

'He was a chemical researcher or whatever they call

it, employed by Runkle's Enterprises, one of those fellows you see in the movies who go about in white coats peering into test tubes. And one day he invented what were afterwards known as Runkle's Magic Midgets, small pills for curing headaches. You've probably come across them.'

'I know them well. Excellent for a hangover, though not of course to be compared with Jeeves's patent pick-me-up. They're very popular at the Drones. I know a dozen fellows who swear by them. There must be a fortune in them.'

'There was. They sell like warm winter woollies in Iceland.'

'Then why is Tuppy short of cash? Didn't he inherit them?'

'Not by a jugful.'

'I don't get it. You speak in riddles, aged relative,' I said, and there was a touch of annoyance in my voice, for if there is one thing that gives me the pip, it is an aunt speaking in riddles. 'If these ruddy midget things belonged to Tuppy's father –'

'L. P. Runkle claimed they didn't. Tuppy's father was working for him on a salary, and the small print in the contract read that all inventions made on Runkle's Enterprises' time became the property of Runkle's Enterprises. So when old Glossop died, he hadn't much to leave his son, while L. P. Runkle went on flourishing like a green bay tree.'

I had never seen a green bay tree, but I gathered what she meant.

'Couldn't Tuppy sue?'

'He would have been bound to lose. A contract is a contract.'

I saw what she meant. It was not unlike that time when she was running that weekly paper of hers, *Milady's Boudoir*, and I contributed to it an article, or piece as it is sometimes called, on What The

Well-Dressed Man Is Wearing. She gave me a packet of cigarettes for it, and it then became her property. I didn't actually get offers for it from France, Germany, Italy, Canada and the United States, but if I had had I couldn't have accepted them. My pal Boko Littleworth, who makes a living by his pen, tells me I ought to have sold her only the first serial rights, but I didn't think of it at the time. One makes these mistakes. What one needs, of course, is an agent.

All the same, I considered that L. P. Runkle ought to have stretched a point and let Tuppy's father get something out of it. I put this to the ancestor, and she agreed with me.

'Of course he ought. Moral obligation.'

'It confirms one's view that this Runkle is a stinker.'

'The stinker supreme. And he tells me he has been tipped off that he's going to get a knighthood in the New Year's Honours.'

'How can they knight a chap like that?'

'Just the sort of chap they do knight. Prominent business man. Big deals. Services to Britain's export trade.'

'But a stinker.'

'Unquestionably a stinker.'

'Then what's he doing here? You usually don't go out of your way to entertain stinkers. Spode, yes. I can understand you letting him infest the premises, much as I disapprove of it. He's making speeches on Ginger's behalf, and according to you doing it rather well. But why Runkle?'

She said 'Ah!', and when I asked her reason for saying 'Ah!', she replied that she was thinking of her subtle cunning, and when I asked what she meant by subtle cunning, she said 'Ah!' again. It looked as if we might go on like this indefinitely, but a moment later, having toddled to the door and opened it and to the French window and peered out, she explained.

'Runkle came here hoping to sell Tom an old silver what not for his collection, and as Tom had vanished and he had come a long way I had to put him up for the night, and at dinner I suddenly had an inspiration. I thought if I got him to stay on and plied him day and night with Anatole's cooking, he might get into mellowed mood.'

She had ceased to speak in riddles. This time I followed her.

'So that you would be able to talk him into slipping Tuppy some of his ill-gotten gains?'

'Exactly. I'm biding my time. When the moment comes, I shall act like lightning. I told him Tom would be back in a day or two, not that he will, because he won't come within fifty miles of the place till I blow the All Clear, so Runkle consented to stay on.'

'And how's it working out?'

'The prospects look good. He mellows more with every meal. Anatole gave us his Mignonette de poulet Petit Duc last night, and he tucked into it like a tapeworm that's been on a diet for weeks. There was no mistaking the gleam in his eyes as he downed the last mouthful. A few more dinners ought to do the trick.'

She left me shortly after this to go and dress for dinner. I, strong in the knowledge that I could get into the soup-and-fish in ten minutes, lingered on, plunged in thought.

Extraordinary how I kept doing that as of even date. It just shows what life is like now. I don't suppose in the old days I would have been plunged in thought more than about once a month.

7

I need scarcely say that Tuppy's hard case, as outlined by the old blood relation, had got right in amongst me. You might suppose that a fellow capable of betting you you couldn't swing yourself across the Drones swimming-bath by the rings and looping the last ring back deserved no consideration, but as I say the agony of that episode had long since abated and it pained me deeply to contemplate the spot he was in. For though I had affected to consider that the ancestor's scheme for melting L. P. Runkle was the goods, I didn't really believe it would work. You don't get anywhere filling with rich foods a bloke who wears a Panama hat like his: the only way of inducing the L. P. Runkle type of man to part with cash is to kidnap him, take him to the cellar beneath the lonely mill and stick lighted matches between his toes. And even then he would probably give you a dud cheque.

The revelation of Tuppy's hard-upness had come as quite a surprise. You know how it is with fellows you're seeing all the time; if you think about their finances at all, you sort of assume they must be all right. It had never occurred to me that Tuppy might be seriously short of doubloons, but I saw now why there had been all this delay in assembling the bishop and assistant clergy and getting the show on the road. I presumed Uncle Tom would brass up if given the green light, he having the stuff in heaping sackfuls, but Tuppy has his pride and would quite properly jib at the idea of being supported by a father-in-law. Of course he really oughtn't to have gone and signed Angela up with his bank balance in such a rocky condition, but love is love. Conquers all, as the fellow said.

Having mused on Tuppy for about five minutes, I changed gears and started musing on Angela, for whom I had always had a cousinly affection. A definitely nice young prune and just the sort to be a good wife, but of course the catch is that you can't be a good wife if the other half of the sketch hasn't enough money to marry you. Practically all you can do is hang around and twiddle your fingers and hope for the best. Weary waiting about sums it up, and the whole lay-out, I felt, must be g. and wormwood for Angela, causing her to bedew her pillow with many a salty tear.

I always find when musing that the thing to do is to bury the face in the hands, because it seems to concentrate thought and keep the mind from wandering off elsewhere. I did this now, and was getting along fairly well, when I suddenly had that uncanny feeling that I was not alone. I sensed a presence, if you would prefer putting it that way, and I had not been mistaken. Removing the hands and looking up, I saw that Madeline Bassett was with me.

It was a nasty shock. I won't say she was the last person I wanted to see, Spode of course heading the list of starters with L. P. Runkle in close attendance, but I would willingly have dispensed with her company. However, I rose courteously, and I don't think there was anything in my manner to suggest that I would have liked to hit her with a brick, for I am pretty inscrutable at all times. Nevertheless, behind my calm front there lurked the uneasiness which always grips me when we meet.

Holding the mistaken view that I am hopelessly in love with her and more or less pining away into a decline, this Bassett never fails to look at me, when our paths cross, with a sort of tender pity, and she was letting me have it now. So melting indeed was her gaze that it was only by reminding myself that she was safely engaged to Spode that I was able to preserve my equanimity and sangfroid. When she had been betrothed to Gussie Fink-Nottle, the peril of her making a switch had always been present, Gussie being the sort of spectacled newt-collecting freak a girl might at any moment get second thoughts about, but there was something so reassuring in her being engaged to Spode. Because, whatever you might think of him, you couldn't get away from it that he was the seventh Earl of Sidcup, and no girl who has managed to hook a seventh Earl with a castle in Shropshire and an income of twenty thousand pounds per annum is lightly going to change her mind about him.

Having given me the look, she spoke, and her voice was like treacle pouring out of a jug.

'Oh, Bertie, how nice to see you again. How are you?'

'I'm fine. How are *you*?'

'I'm fine.'

'That's fine. How's your father?'

'He's fine.'

I was sorry to hear this. My relations with Sir Watkyn Bassett were such that a more welcome piece of news would have been that he had contracted bubonic plague and wasn't expected to recover.

'I heard you were here,' I said.

'Yes, I'm here.'

'So I heard. You're looking well.'

'Oh, I'm very, very well, and oh so happy.'

'That's good.'

'I wake up each morning to the new day, and I know it's going to be the best day that ever was. Today I danced on the lawn before breakfast, and then I went round the garden saying good morning to the flowers. There was a sweet black cat asleep on one of the flower beds. I picked it up and danced with it.'

I didn't tell her so, but she couldn't have made a worse social gaffe. If there is one thing Augustus, the cat to whom she referred, hates, it's having his sleep disturbed. He must have cursed freely, though probably in a drowsy undertone. I suppose she thought he was purring.

She had paused, seeming to expect some comment on her fatheaded behaviour, so I said:

'Euphoria.'

'I what?'

'That's what it's called, Jeeves tells me, feeling like that.'

'Oh, I see. I just call it being happy, happy, happy.'

Having said which, she gave a start, quivered and put a hand up to her face as if she were having a screen test and had been told to register remorse.

'Oh, Bertie!'

'Hullo?'

'I'm so sorry.'

'Eh?'

'It was so tactless of me to go on about my happiness. I should have remembered how different it was for you. I saw your face twist with pain as I came in and I can't tell you how sorry I am to think that it is I who have caused it. Life is not easy, is it?'

'Not very.'

'Difficult.'

'In spots.'

'The only thing is to be brave.'

'That's about it.'

'You must not lose courage. Who knows? Consolation may be waiting for you somewhere. Some day you will meet someone who will make you forget you ever loved me. No, not quite that. I think I shall always be a fragrant memory, always something deep in your heart that will be with you like a gentle, tender ghost as you watch the sunset on summer evenings while the little birds sing their off-to-bed songs in the shrubbery.'

'I wouldn't be surprised,' I said, for one simply has to say the civil thing. 'You look a bit damp,' I added, changing the subject. 'Was it raining when you were out?'

'A little, but I didn't mind. I was saying good-night to the flowers.'

'Oh, you say good-night to them, too?'

'Of course. Their poor little feelings would be so hurt if I didn't.'

'Wise of you to come in. Might have got lumbago.'

'That was not why I came in. I saw you through the window, and I had a question to ask you. A very, very serious question.'

'Oh, yes?'

'But it's so difficult to know how to put it. I shall have to ask it as they do in books. You know what they say in books.'

'What who say in books?'

'Detectives and people like that. Bertie, are you going straight now?'

'I beg your pardon?'

'You know what I mean. Have you given up stealing things?'

I laughed one of those gay debonair ones.

'Oh, absolutely.'

'I'm so glad. You don't feel the urge any more? You've conquered the craving? I told Daddy it was just a kind of illness. I said you couldn't help yourself.'

I remembered her submitting this theory to him . . . I was hiding behind a sofa at the time, a thing I have been compelled to do rather oftener than I could wish . . . and Sir Watkyn had replied in what I thought dubious taste that it was precisely my habit of helping myself to everything I could lay my hands on that he was criticizing.

Another girl might have left it at that, but not M. Bassett. She was all eager curiosity.

'Did you have psychiatric treatment? Or was it will power?'

'Just will power.'

'How splendid. I'm so proud of you. It must have been a terrible struggle.'

'Oh, so-so.'

'I shall write to Daddy and tell him –'

Here she paused and put a hand to her left eye, and it was easy for a man of my discernment to see what had happened. The French window being open, gnats in fairly large numbers had been coming through and flitting to and fro. It's a thing one always has to budget for in the English countryside. In America they have screens, of course, which make flying objects feel pretty nonplussed, but these have never caught on in England and the gnats have it more or less their own way. They horse around and now and then get into people's eyes. One of these, it was evident, had now got into Madeline's.

I would be the last to deny that Bertram Wooster has his limitations, but in one field of endeavour I am pre-eminent. In the matter of taking things out of eyes I yield to no one. I know what to say and what to do.

Counselling her not to rub it, I advanced handkerchief in hand.

I remember going into the technique of operations of this kind with Gussie Fink-Nottle at Totleigh when he had removed a fly from the eye of Stephanie Byng, now the Reverend Mrs Stinker Pinker, and we were in agreement that success could be achieved only by placing a hand under the patient's chin in order to steady the head. Omit this preliminary and your efforts are bootless. My first move, accordingly, was to do so and it was characteristic of Spode that he should have chosen this moment to join us, just when we twain were in what you might call close juxtaposition.

I confess that there have been times when I have felt

more at my ease. Spode, in addition to being constructed on the lines of a rather oversized gorilla, has a disposition like that of a short-tempered tiger of the jungle and a nasty mind which leads him to fall a ready prey to what I have heard Jeeves call the green-eyed monster which doth mock the meat it feeds on – viz. jealousy. Such a man, finding you steadying the head of the girl he loves, is always extremely likely to start trying to ascertain the colour of your insides, and to avert this I greeted him with what nonchalance I could muster.

'Oh, hullo, Spode old chap, I mean Lord Sidcup old chap. Here we all are, what. Jeeves told me you were here, and Aunt Dahlia says you've been knocking the voting public base over apex with your oratory in the Conservative interest. Must be wonderful to be able to do that. It's a gift, of course. Some have it, some haven't. I couldn't address a political meeting to please a dying grandmother. I should stand there opening and shutting my mouth like a goldfish. You, on the other hand, just clear your throat and the golden words come pouring out like syrup. I admire you enormously.'

Conciliatory, I think you'll agree. I could hardly have given him the old salve with a more liberal hand, and one might have expected him to simper, shuffle his feet and mumble 'Awfully nice of you to say so' or something along those lines. Instead of which, all he did was come back at me with a guttural sound like an opera basso choking on a fishbone and I had to sustain the burden of the conversation by myself.

'I've just been taking a gnat out of Madeline's eye.'

'Oh?'

'Dangerous devils, these gnats. Require skilled handling.'

'Oh?'

'Everything's back to normal now, I think.'

'Yes, thank you ever so much, Bertie.'

It was Madeline who said this, not Spode. He continued to gaze at me bleakly. She went on harping on the thing.

'Bertie's so clever.'

'Oh?'

'I don't know what I would have done without him.'

'Oh?'

'He showed wonderful presence of mind.'

'Oh?'

'I feel so sorry, though, for the poor little gnat.'

'It asked for it,' I pointed out. 'It was unquestionably the aggressor.'

'Yes, I suppose that's true, but . . .' The clock on the mantelpiece caught her now de-gnatted eye, and she uttered an agitated squeak. 'Oh, my goodness, is that the time? I must rush.'

She buzzed off, and I was on the point of doing the same, when Spode detained me with a curt 'One moment'. There are all sorts of ways of saying 'One moment'. This was one of the nastier ones, spoken with an unpleasant rasping note in the voice.

'I want a word with you, Wooster.'

I am never anxious to chat with Spode, but if I had been sure that he merely wanted to go on saying 'Oh?', I would have been willing to listen. Something, however, seemed to tell me that he was about to give evidence of a wider vocabulary, and I edged towards the door.

'Some other time, don't you think?'

'Not some ruddy other time. Now.'

'I shall be late for dinner.'

'You can't be too late for me. And if you get your teeth knocked down your throat, as you will if you don't listen attentively to what I have to say, you won't be able to eat any dinner.'

This seemed plausible. I decided to lend him an ear, as the expression is. 'Say on,' I said, and he said on, lowering his voice to a sort of rumbling growl which made him difficult to follow. However, I caught the word 'read' and the word 'book' and perked up a bit. If this was going to be a literary discussion, I didn't mind exchanging views.

'Book?' I said.

'Book.'

'You want me to recommend you a good book? Well, of course, it depends on what you like. Jeeves, for instance, is never happier than when curled up with his Spinoza or his Shakespeare. I, on the other hand, go in mostly for who-dun-its and novels of suspense. For the who-dun-it Agatha Christie is always a safe bet. For the novel of suspense . . .'

Here I paused, for he had called me an opprobrious name and told me to stop babbling, and it is always my policy to stop babbling when a man eight foot six in height and broad in proportion tells me to. I went into the silence, and he continued to say on.

'I said that I could read you like a book, Wooster. I know what your game is.'

'I don't understand you, Lord Sidcup.'

'Then you must be as big an ass as you look, which is saying a good deal. I am referring to your behaviour towards my fiancée. I come into this room and I find you fondling her face.'

I had to correct him here. One likes to get these things straight.

'Only her chin.'

'Pah!' he said, or something that sounded like that.

'And I had to get a grip on it in order to extract the gnat from her eye. I was merely steadying it.'

'You were steadying it gloatingly.'

'I wasn't!'

'Pardon me. I have eyes and can see when a man is steadying a chin gloatingly and when he isn't. You were obviously delighted to have an excuse for soiling her chin with your foul fingers.'

'You are wrong, Lord Spodecup.'

'And, as I say, I know what your game is. You are trying to undermine me, to win her from me with your insidious guile, and what I want to impress upon you with all the emphasis at my disposal is that if anything of this sort is going to occur again, you would do well to take out an accident policy with some good insurance company at the earliest possible date. You probably think that being a guest in your aunt's house I would hesitate to butter you over the front lawn and dance on the fragments in hobnailed boots, but you are mistaken. It will be a genuine pleasure. By an odd coincidence I brought a pair of hobnailed boots with me!'

So saying, and recognizing a good exit line when he saw one, he strode out, and after an interval of tense meditation I followed him. Repairing to my bedroom, I found Jeeves there, looking reproachful. He knows I can dress for dinner in ten minutes, but regards haste askance, for he thinks it results in a tie which, even if adequate, falls short of the perfect butterfly effect.

I ignored the silent rebuke in his eyes. After meeting Spode's eyes, I was dashed if I was going to be intimidated by Jeeves's.

'Jeeves,' I said, 'you're fairly well up in Hymns Ancient and Modern, I should imagine. Who were the fellows in the hymn who used to prowl and prowl around?'

'The troops of Midian, sir.'

'That's right. Was Spode mentioned as one of them?'

'Sir?'

'I ask because he's prowling around as if Midian was his home town. Let me tell you all about it.'

'I fear it will not be feasible, sir. The gong is sounding.'

'So it is. Who's sounding it? You said Seppings was in bed.'

'The parlourmaid, sir, deputizing for Mr Seppings.'

'I like her wrist work. Well, I'll tell you later.'

'Very good, sir. Pardon me, your tie.'

'What's wrong with it?'

'Everything, sir. If you will allow me.'

'All right, go ahead. But I can't help asking myself if ties really matter at a time like this.'

'There is no time when ties do not matter, sir.'

My mood was sombre as I went down to dinner. Anatole, I was thinking, would no doubt give us of his best, possibly his *Timbale de ris de veau Toulousaine* or his *Sylphides à la crème d'écrevisses*, but Spode would be there and Madeline would be there and Florence would be there and L. P. Runkle would be there.

There was, I reflected, always something.

8

It has been well said of Bertram Wooster that when he sets his hand to the plough he does not stop to pick daisies and let the grass grow under his feet. Many men in my position, having undertaken to canvass for a friend anxious to get into Parliament, would have waited till after lunch next day to get rolling, saying to themselves Oh, what difference do a few hours make and going off to the billiard-room for a game or two of snooker. I, in sharp contradistinction as I have heard Jeeves call it, was on my way shortly after breakfast. It can't have been much more than a quarter to eleven when, fortified by a couple of kippers, toast, marmalade and three cups of coffee, I might have been observed approaching a row of houses down by the river to which someone with a flair for the *mot juste* had given the name of River Row. From long acquaintance with the town I knew that this was one of the posher parts of Market Snodsbury, stiff with householders likely to favour the Conservative cause, and it was for that reason that I was making it my first port of call. No sense, I mean, in starting off with the less highly priced localities where everybody was bound to vote Labour and would not only turn a deaf ear to one's reasoning but might even bung a brick at one. Ginger no doubt had a special posse of tough supporters, talking and spitting out of the side of their mouths, and they would attend to the brick-bunging portion of the electorate.

Jeeves was at my side, but whereas I had selected Number One as my objective, his intention was to push on to Number Two. I would then give Number Three the treatment, while he did the same to Number Four. Talking it over, we had decided that if we made it a double act and blew into a house together, it might give the occupant the impression that he was receiving a visit from the plain clothes police and excite him unduly. Many of the men who live in places like River Row have a tendency to apoplectic fits as the result of high living, and a voter expiring on the floor from shock means a voter less on the voting list. One has to think of these things.

'What beats me, Jeeves,' I said, for I was in thoughtful mood, 'is why people don't object to somebody they don't know from Adam muscling into their homes without a . . . without a what? It's on the tip of my tongue.'

'A With-your-leave or a By-your-leave, sir?'

'That's right. Without a With-your-leave or a By-your-leave and telling them which way to vote. Taking a liberty, it strikes me as.'

'It is the custom at election time, sir. Custom reconciles us to everything, a wise man once said.'

'Shakespeare?'

'Burke, sir. You will find the apothegm in his *On The Sublime And Beautiful*. I think the electors, conditioned by many years of canvassing, would be disappointed if nobody called on them.'

'So we shall be bringing a ray of sunshine into their drab lives?'

'Something on that order, sir.'

'Well, you may be right. Have you ever done this sort of thing before?'

'Once or twice, sir, before I entered your employment.'

'What were your methods?'

'I outlined as briefly as possible the main facets of my argument, bade my auditors goodbye, and withdrew.'

'No preliminaries?'

'Sir?'

'You didn't make a speech of any sort before getting down to brass tacks? No mention of Burke or Shakespeare or the poet Burns?'

'No, sir. It might have caused exasperation.'

I disagreed with him. I felt that he was on the wrong track altogether and couldn't expect anything in the nature of a triumph at Number Two. There is probably nothing a voter enjoys more than hearing the latest about Burke and his *On The Sublime And Beautiful*, and here he was, deliberately chucking away the advantages his learning gave him. I had half a mind to draw his attention to the Parable of the Talents, with which I had become familiar when doing research for that Scripture Knowledge prize I won at school. Time, however, was getting along, so I passed it up. But I told him I thought he was mistaken. Preliminaries, I maintained, were of the essence. Breaking the ice is what it's called. I mean, you can't just barge in on a perfect stranger and get off the mark with an abrupt 'Hoy there. I hope you're going to vote for my candidate!' How much better to say 'Good morning, sir. I can see at a glance that you are a man of culture, probably never happier than when reading your Burke. I wonder if you are familiar with his *On The Sublime And Beautiful*?' Then away you go, off to a nice start.

'You must have an approach,' I said. 'I myself am all for the jolly, genial. I propose, on meeting my householder, to begin with a jovial "Hullo there, Mr Whatever-it-is, hullo there", thus ingratiating myself with him from the kick-off. I shall then tell him a funny story. Then, and only then, will I get to the nub – waiting, of course, till he has stopped laughing. I can't fail.'

'I am sure you will not, sir. The system would not suit me, but it is merely a matter of personal taste.'

'The psychology of the individual, what?'

'Precisely, sir. By different methods different men excel.'

'Burke?'

'Charles Churchill, sir, a poet who flourished in the early eighteenth century. The words occur in his *Epistle To William Hogarth*.'

We halted. Cutting out a good pace, we had arrived at the door of Number One. I pressed the bell.

'Zero hour, Jeeves,' I said gravely.

'Yes, sir.'

'Carry on.'

'Very good, sir.'

'Heaven speed your canvassing.'

'Thank you, sir.'

'And mine.'

'Yes, sir.'

He pushed along and mounted the steps of Number Two, leaving me feeling rather as I had done in my younger days at a clergyman uncle's place in Kent when about to compete in the Choir Boys Bicycle Handicap open to all those whose voices had not broken by the first Sunday in Epiphany – nervous, but full of the will to win.

The door opened as I was running through the high spots of the laughable story I planned to unleash when I got inside. A maid was standing there, and conceive my emotion when I recognized her as one who had held office under Aunt Dahlia the last time I had enjoyed the latter's hospitality; the one with whom, the old sweats will recall, I had chewed the fat on the subject of the cat Augustus and his tendency to pass his days in sleep instead of bustling about and catching mice.

The sight of her friendly face was like a tonic. My morale, which had begun to sag a bit after Jeeves had left me, rose sharply, closing at nearly par. I felt that even if the fellow I was going to see kicked me downstairs, she would be there to show me out and tell me that these things are sent to try us, with the general idea of making us more spiritual.

'Why, hullo!' I said.

'Good morning, sir.'

'We meet again.'

'Yes, sir.'

'You remember me?'

'Oh yes, sir.'

'And you have not forgotten Augustus?'

'Oh no, sir.'

'He's still as lethargic as ever. He joined me at breakfast this morning. Just managed to keep awake while getting outside his portion of kipper, then fell into a dreamless sleep at the end of the bed with his head hanging down. So you have resigned your portfolio at Aunt Dahlia's since we last met. Too bad. We shall all miss you. Do you like it here?'

'Oh yes, sir.'

'That's the spirit. Well, getting down to business, I've come to see your boss on a matter of considerable importance. What sort of chap is he? Not too short-tempered? Not too apt to be cross with callers, I hope?'

'It isn't a gentleman, sir, it's a lady. Mrs McCorkadale.'

This chipped quite a bit off the euphoria I was feeling. I had been relying on the story I had prepared to put me over with a bang, carrying me safely through the first awkward moments when the fellow you've called on without an invitation is staring at you as if wondering to what he owes the honour of this visit, and now it would have to remain untold. It was one I had heard from Catsmeat Potter-Pirbright at the Drones and it was essentially a *conte* whose spiritual home was the smoking-room of a London club or the men's wash-room on an American train – in short, one by no means adapted to the ears of the gentle sex; especially a member of that sex who probably ran the local Watch Committee.

It was, consequently, a somewhat damped Bertram Wooster whom the maid ushered into the drawing-room, and my pep was in no way augmented by the first sight I had of mine hostess. Mrs McCorkadale was what I would call a grim woman. Not so grim as my Aunt Agatha, perhaps, for that could hardly be expected, but certainly well up in the class of Jael the wife of Heber and the Madame Whoever-it-was who used to sit and knit at the foot of the guillotine during the French Revolution. She had a beaky nose, tight thin lips, and her eye could have been used for splitting logs in the teak forests of Borneo. Seeing her steadily and seeing her whole, as the expression is, one marvelled at the intrepidity of Mr McCorkadale in marrying her – a man obviously whom nothing could daunt.

However, I had come there to be jolly and genial, and jolly and genial I was resolved to be. Actors will tell you that on these occasions, when the soul is a-twitter and the nervous system not like mother makes it, the thing to do is to take a deep breath. I took three, and immediately felt much better.

'Good morning, good morning, good morning,' I said. 'Good morning,' I added, rubbing it in, for it was my policy to let there be no stint.

'Good morning,' she replied, and one might have totted things up as so far, so good. But if I said she said it cordially, I would be deceiving my public. The impression I got was that the sight of me hurt her in some sensitive spot. The woman, it was plain, shared Spode's view of what was needed to make England a land fit for heroes to live in.

Not being able to uncork the story and finding the way her eye was going through me like a dose of salts more than a little trying to my already dented sangfroid, I might have had some difficulty in getting the conversation going, but fortunately I was full of good material just waiting to be decanted. Over an after-dinner smoke on the previous night Ginger had filled me in on what his crowd proposed to do when they got down to it. They were going, he said, to cut taxes to the bone, straighten out our foreign policy, double our export trade, have two cars in the garage and two chickens in the pot for everyone and give the pound the shot in the arm it had been clamouring for for years. Than which, we both agreed, nothing could be sweeter, and I saw no reason to suppose that the McCorkadale gargoyle would not feel the same. I began, therefore, by asking her if she had a vote, and she said Yes, of course, and I said Well, that was fine, because if she hadn't had, the point of my arguments would have been largely lost.

'An excellent thing, I've always thought, giving women the vote,' I proceeded heartily, and she said – rather nastily, it seemed to me – that she was glad I approved. 'When you cast yours, if cast is the word I want, I strongly advise you to cast it in favour of Ginger Winship.'

'On what do you base that advice?'

She couldn't have given me a better cue. She had handed it to me on a plate with watercress round it. Like a flash I went into my sales talk, mentioning Ginger's attitude towards taxes, our foreign policy, our export trade, cars in the garage, chickens in the pot and first aid for the poor old pound, and was shocked to observe an entire absence of enthusiasm on her part. Not a ripple appeared on the stern and rockbound coast of her map. She looked like Aunt Agatha listening to the boy Wooster trying to explain away a drawing-room window broken by a cricket ball.

I pressed her closely, or do I mean keenly.

'You want taxes cut, don't you?'

'I do.'

'And our foreign policy bumped up?'

'Certainly.'

'And our exports doubled and a stick of dynamite put under the pound? I'll bet you do. Then vote for Ginger Winship, the man who with his hand on the helm of the ship of state will steer England to prosperity and happiness, bringing back once more the spacious days of Good Queen Bess.' This was a line of talk that Jeeves had roughed out for my use. There was also some rather good stuff about this sceptred isle and this other Eden, demi-something, but I had forgotten it. 'You can't say that wouldn't be nice,' I said.

A moment before, I wouldn't have thought it possible that she could look more like Aunt Agatha than she had been doing, but she now achieved this breathtaking feat. She sniffed, if not snorted, and spoke as follows:

'Young man, don't be idiotic. Hand on the helm of the ship of state, indeed! If Mr Winship performs the miracle of winning this election, which he won't, he will be an ordinary humble back-bencher, doing nothing more notable than saying "Hear, hear" when his superiors are speaking and "Oh" and "Question" when the opposition have the floor. As,' she went on, 'I shall if I win this election, as I intend to.'

I blinked. A sharp 'Whatwasthatyousaid?' escaped my lips, and she proceeded to explain or, as Jeeves would say, elucidate.

'You are not very quick at noticing things, are you? I imagine not, or you would have seen that Market Snodsbury is liberally plastered with posters bearing the words "Vote for McCorkadale". An abrupt way of putting it, but one that is certainly successful in conveying its meaning.'

It was a blow, I confess, and I swayed beneath it like an aspen, if aspens are those things that sway. The Woosters can take a good deal, but only so much. My most coherent thought at the moment was that it was just like my luck, when I sallied forth as a canvasser, to collide first crack out of the box with the rival candidate. I also had the feeling that if Jeeves had taken on Number One instead of Number Two, he would probably have persuaded Ma McCorkadale to vote against herself.

I suppose if you had asked Napoleon how he had managed to get out of Moscow, he would have been a bit vague about it, and it was the same with me. I found myself on the front steps with only a sketchy notion of how I had got there, and I was in the poorest of shapes. To try to restore the shattered system I lit a cigarette and had begun to puff, when a cheery voice hailed me and I became aware that some foreign substance was sharing my doorstep. 'Hullo, Wooster old chap' it was saying and, the mists clearing from before my eyes, I saw that it was Bingley.

I gave the blighter a distant look. Knowing that this blot on the species resided in Market Snodsbury, I had foreseen that I might run into him sooner or later, so I was not surprised to see him. But I certainly wasn't pleased. The last thing I wanted in the delicate state to which the McCorkadale had reduced me was conversation with a man who set cottages on fire and chased the hand that fed him hither and thither with a carving knife.

He was as unduly intimate, forward, bold, intrusive and deficient in due respect as he had been at the Junior Ganymede. He gave my back a cordial slap and would, I think, have prodded me in the ribs if it had occurred to him. You wouldn't have thought that carving knives had ever come between us.

'And what are *you* doing in these parts, cocky?' he asked.

I said I was visiting my aunt Mrs Travers, who had a house in the vicinity, and he said he knew the place, though he had never met the old geezer to whom I referred.

'I've seen her around. Red-faced old girl, isn't she?'

'Fairly vermilion.'

'High blood pressure, probably.'

'Or caused by going in a lot for hunting. It chaps the cheeks.'

'Different from a barmaid. She cheeks the chaps.'

If he had supposed that his crude humour would get so much as a simper out of me, he was disappointed. I preserved the cold aloofness of a Wednesday matinée audience, and he proceeded.

'Yes, that might be it. She looks a sport. Making a long stay?'

'I don't know,' I said, for the length of my visits to the old ancestor is always uncertain. So much depends on whether she throws me out or not. 'Actually I'm here to canvass for the Conservative candidate. He's a pal of mine.'

He whistled sharply. He had been looking repulsive and cheerful; he now looked repulsive and grave. Seeming to realize that he had omitted a social gesture, he prodded me in the ribs.

'You're wasting your time, Wooster, old man,' he said. 'He hasn't an earthly.'

'No?' I quavered. It was simply one man's opinion, of course, but the earnestness with which he had spoken was unquestionably impressive. 'What makes you think that?'

'Never you mind what makes me think it. Take my word for it. If you're sensible, you'll phone your bookie and have a big bet on McCorkadale. You'll never regret it. You'll come to me later and thank me for the tip with tears in your –'

At some point in this formal interchange of thoughts by spoken word, as Jeeves's *Dictionary of Synonyms* puts it, he must have pressed the bell, for at this moment the door opened and my old buddy the maid appeared. Quickly adding the word 'eyes', he turned to her.

'Mrs McCorkadale in, dear?' he asked, and having been responded to in the affirmative he left me, and I headed for home. I ought, of course, to have carried on along River Row, taking the odd numbers while Jeeves attended to the even, but I didn't feel in the vein.

I was uneasy. You might say, if you happened to know the word, that the prognostications of a human wart like Bingley deserved little credence, but he had spoken with such conviction, so like someone who has heard something, that I couldn't pass them off with a light laugh.

Brooding tensely, I reached the old homestead and found the ancestor lying on a chaise longue, doing the *Observer* crossword puzzle.

9

There was a time when this worthy housewife, tackling the *Observer* crossword puzzle, would snort and tear her hair and fill the air with strange oaths picked up from cronies on the hunting field, but consistent inability to solve more than about an eighth of the clues has brought a sort of dull resignation and today she merely sits and stares at it, knowing that however much she licks the end of her pencil little or no business will result.

As I came in, I heard her mutter, soliloquizing like someone in Shakespeare, 'Measured tread of saint round St Paul's, for God's sake', seeming to indicate that she had come up against a hot one, and I think it was a relief to her to become aware that her favourite nephew was at her side and that she could conscientiously abandon her distasteful task, for she looked up and greeted me cheerily. She wears tortoiseshell-rimmed spectacles for reading which make her look like a fish in an aquarium. She peered at me through these.

'Hullo, my bounding Bertie.'

'Good morning, old ancestor.'

'Up already?'

'I have been up some time.'

'Then why aren't you out canvassing? And why are you looking like something the cat brought in?'

I winced. I had not intended to disclose the recent past, but with an aunt's perception she had somehow spotted that in some manner I had passed through the furnace and she would go on probing and questioning till I came clean. Any capable aunt can give Scotland Yard inspectors strokes and bisques in the matter of interrogating a suspect, and I knew that all attempts at concealment would be fruitless. Or is it bootless? I would have to check with Jeeves.

'I am looking like something the cat brought in because I am feeling like something the c.b. in,' I said. 'Aged relative, I have a strange story to relate. Do you know a local blister of the name of Mrs McCorkadale?'

'Who lives in River Row?'

'That's the one.'

'She's a barrister.'

'She looks it.'

'You've met her?'

'I've met her.'

'She's Ginger's opponent in this election.'

'I know. Is Mr McCorkadale still alive?'

'Died years ago. He got run over by a municipal tram.'

'I don't blame him. I'd have done the same myself in his place. It's the only course to pursue when you're married to a woman like that.'

'How did you meet her?'

'I called on her to urge her to vote for Ginger,' I said, and in a few broken words I related my strange story.

It went well. In fact, it went like a breeze. Myself, I was unable to see anything humorous in it, but there was no doubt about it entertaining the blood relation. She guffawed more liberally than I had ever heard a woman guffaw. If there had been an aisle, she would have rolled in it. I couldn't help feeling how ironical it was that, having failed so often to be well received when telling a funny story, I should have aroused such gales of mirth with one that was so essentially tragic.

While she was still giving her impersonation of a hyena which has just heard a good one from another hyena, Spode came in, choosing the wrong moment as usual. One never wants to see Spode, but least of all when someone is having a hearty laugh at your expense.

'I'm looking for the notes for my speech tomorrow,' he said. 'Hullo, what's the joke?'

Convulsed as she was, it was not easy for the ancestor to articulate, but she managed a couple of words.

'It's Bertie.'

'Oh?' said Spode, looking at me as if he found it difficult to believe that any word or act of mine could excite mirth and not horror and disgust.

'He's just been calling on Mrs McCorkadale.'

'Oh?'

'And asking her to vote for Ginger Winship.'

'Oh?' said Spode again. I have already indicated that he was a compulsive Oh-sayer. 'Well, it is what I would have expected of him,' and with another look in which scorn and animosity were nicely blended and a word to the effect that he might have left those notes in the summerhouse by the lake he removed his distasteful presence.

That he and I were not on Damon and Pythias terms seemed to have impressed itself on the aged relative. She switched off the hyena sound effects.

'Not a bonhomous type, Spode.'

'No.'

'He doesn't like you.'

'No.'

'And I don't think he likes me.'

'No,' I said, and it occurred to me, for the Woosters are essentially fairminded, that it was hardly for me to criticize Spode's Oh's when my No's were equally frequent. Why beholdest thou the mote that is in thy brother's eye, but considerest not the beam that is in thine own eye, Wooster? I found myself asking myself, it having been one of the many good things I had picked up in my researches when I won that Scripture Knowledge prize.

'Does he like anyone?' said the relative. 'Except, presumably, Madeline Bassett.'

'He seems fond of L. P. Runkle.'

'What makes you think that?'

'I overheard them exchanging confidences.'

'Oh?' said the relative, for these things are catching. 'Well, I suppose one ought not to be surprised. Birds of a feather –'

'Flock together?'

'Exactly. And even the dregs of pond life fraternize with other dregs of pond life. By the way, remind me to tell you something about L. P. Runkle.'

'Right ho.'

'We will come to L. P. Runkle later. This animosity of Spode's, is it just the memory of old Totleigh days, or have you done anything lately to incur his displeasure?'

This time I had no hesitation in telling her all. I felt she would be sympathetic. I laid the facts before her with every confidence that an aunt's condolences would result.

'There was this gnat.'

'I don't follow you.'

'I had to rally round.'

'You've still lost me.'

'Spode didn't like it.'

'So he doesn't like gnats either. Which gnat? What gnat? Will you get on with your story, curse you, starting at the beginning and carrying on to the end.'

'Certainly, if you wish. Here is the scenario.'

I told her about the gnat in Madeline's eye, the part I had played in restoring her vision to mid-season form and the exception Spode had taken to my well-meant efforts. She whistled. Everyone seemed to be whistling at me today. Even the recent maid on recognizing me had puckered up her lips as if about to.

'I wouldn't do that sort of thing again,' she said.

'If the necessity arose I would have no option.'

'Then you'd better get one as soon as possible.

Because if you keep on taking things out of Madeline's
eye, you may have to marry the girl.'

'But surely the peril has passed now that she's engaged
to Spode.'

'I don't know so much. I think there's some trouble
between Spode and Madeline.'

I would be surprised to learn that in the whole W.1
postal section of London there is a man more capable
than Bertram Wooster of bearing up with a stiff upper lip
under what I have heard Jeeves call the slings and arrows
of outrageous fortune; but at these frightful words I
confess that I went into my old aspen routine even more
wholeheartedly than I had done during my get-together
with the relict of the late McCorkadale.

And not without reason. My whole foreign policy was
based on the supposition that the solidarity of these two
consenting adults was something that couldn't be
broken or even cracked. He, on his own statement, had
worshipped her since she was so high, while she, as I
have already recorded, would not lightly throw a man of
his eligibility into the discard. If ever there was a union
which you could have betted with perfect confidence
would culminate in a golden wedding with all the
trimmings, this was the one.

'Trouble?' I whispered hoarsely. 'You mean there's a
what-d'you-call-it?'

'What would that be?'

'A rift within the lute which widens soon and makes
the music mute. Not my own, Jeeves's.'

'The evidence points in that direction. At dinner last
night I noticed that he was refusing Anatole's best,
while she looked wan and saintlike and crumbled bread.
And talking of Anatole's best, what I wanted to tell you
about L. P. Runkle was that zero hour is approaching. I
am crouching for my spring and have strong hopes that
Tuppy will soon be in the money.'

I clicked the tongue. Nobody could be keener than I

on seeing Tuppy dip into L. P. Runkle's millions, but this was no time to change the subject.

'Never mind about Tuppy for the moment. Concentrate on the sticky affairs of Bertram Wilberforce Wooster.'

'Wilberforce,' she murmured, as far as a woman of her outstanding lung power could murmur. 'Did I ever tell you how you got that label? It was your father's doing. The day before you were lugged to the font looking like a minor actor playing a bit part in a gangster film he won a packet on an outsider in the Grand National called that, and he insisted on you carrying on the name. Tough on you, but we all have our cross to bear. Your Uncle Tom's second name is Portarlington, and I came within an ace of being christened Phyllis.'

I rapped her sharply on the top-knot with a paper-knife of Oriental design, the sort that people in novels of suspense are always getting stabbed in the back with.

'Don't wander from the *res*. The fact that you nearly got christened Phyllis will, no doubt, figure in your autobiography, but we need not discuss it now. What we are talking about is the ghastly peril that confronts me if the Madeline–Spode axis blows a fuse.'

'You mean that if she breaks her engagement, you will have to fill the vacuum?'

'Exactly.'

'She won't. Not a chance.'

'But you said – '

'I only wanted to emphasize my warning to you not to keep on taking gnats out of Madeline's eyes. Perhaps I overdid it.'

'You chilled me to the marrow.'

'Sorry I was so dramatic. You needn't worry. They've only had a lovers' tiff such as occurs with the mushiest couples.'

'What about?'

'How do I know? Perhaps he queried her statement that the stars were God's daisy chain.'

I had to admit that there was something in this theory. Madeline's breach with Gussie Fink-Nottle had been caused by her drawing his attention to the sunset and saying sunsets always made her think of the Blessed Damozel leaning out from the gold bar of heaven, and he said, 'Who?' and she said, 'The Blessed Damozel', and he said, 'Never heard of her', adding that sunsets made him sick, and so did the Blessed Damozel. A girl with her outlook would be bound to be touchy about stars and daisy chains.

'It's probably over by now,' said the ancestor. 'All the same, you'd better keep away from the girl. Spode's an impulsive man. He might slosh you.'

'He said he would.'

'He used the word slosh?'

'No, but he assured me he would butter me over the front lawn and dance on the remains with hobnailed boots.'

'Much the same thing. So I would be careful if I were you. Treat her with distant civility. If you see any more gnats headed in her direction, hold their coats and wish them luck, but restrain the impulse to mix in.'

'I will.'

'I hope I have relieved your fears?'

'You have, old flesh-and-blood.'

'Then why the furrows in your brow?'

'Oh, those? It's Ginger.'

'What's Ginger?'

'He's why my brow is furrowed.'

It shows how profoundly the thought of Madeline Bassett possibly coming into circulation again had moved me that it was only now that I had remembered Bingley and what he had said about the certainty of Ginger finishing as an also-ran in the election. I burned with shame and remorse that I should have allowed my

personal troubles to make me shove him down to the
foot of the agenda paper in this scurvy manner. Long ere
this I ought to have been inviting Aunt Dahlia's views
on his prospects. Not doing so amounted to letting a pal
down, a thing I pride myself on never being guilty of.
Little wonder that I b.'d with s. and r.

I hastened to make amends, if those are what you
make when you have done the dirty on a fellow you love
like a brother.

'Did I ever mention a bloke called Bingley to you?'

'If you did. I've forgotten.'

'He was my personal attendant for a brief space when
Jeeves and I differed about me playing the banjolele.
That time when I had a cottage down at Chufnell Regis.'

'Oh yes, he set it on fire, didn't he?'

'While tight as an owl. It was burned to a cinder, as
was my banjolele.'

'I've got him placed now. What about him?'

'He lives in Market Snodsbury. I met him this
morning and happened to mention that I was canvassing
for Ginger.'

'If you can call it canvassing.'

'And he told me I was wasting my time. He advised
me to have a substantial bet on Ma McCorkadale. He
said Ginger hadn't an earthly.'

'He's a fool.'

'I must say I've always thought so, but he spoke as if
he had inside information.'

'What on earth information could he have? An
election isn't a horse race where you get tips from the
stable cat. I don't say it may not be a close thing, but
Ginger ought to win all right. He has a secret weapon.'

'Repeat that, if you wouldn't mind. I don't think I got
it.'

'Ginger defies competition because he has a secret
weapon.'

'Which is?'

'Spode.'

'Spode?'

'My lord Sidcup. Have you ever heard him speak?'

'I did just now.'

'In public, fool.'

'Oh, in public. No, I haven't.'

'He's a terrific orator, as I told you, only you've probably forgotten.'

This seemed likely enough to me. Spode at one time had been one of those Dictators, going about at the head of a band of supporters in footer shorts shouting '*Heil* Spode', and to succeed in that line you have to be able to make speeches.

'You aren't fond of him, nor am I, but nobody can deny that he's eloquent. Audiences hang on his every word, and when he's finished cheer him to the echo.'

I nodded. I had had the same experience myself when singing 'The Yeoman's Wedding Song' at village concerts. Two or three encores sometimes, even when I blew up in the words and had to fill in with 'Ding dong, ding dong, ding dong, I hurry along'. I began to feel easier in my mind. I told her this, and she said 'Your *what*?'

'You have put new heart into me, old blood relation,' I said, ignoring the crack. 'You see, it means everything to him to win this election.'

'Is he so bent on representing Market Snodsbury in the Westminster menagerie?'

'It isn't that so much. Left to himself, I imagine he could take Parliament or leave it alone. But he thinks Florence will give him the bum's rush if he loses.'

'He's probably right. She can't stand a loser.'

'So he told me. Remember what happened to Percy Gorringe.'

'And others. England is strewn with ex-fiancés whom she bounced because they didn't come up to her specifications. Dozens of them. I believe they form clubs and societies.'

'Perhaps calling themselves the Old Florentians.'

'And having an annual dinner!'

We mused on Florence for awhile; then she said she ought to be going to confer with Anatole about dinner tonight, urging him to dish up something special. It was vital, she said, that he should excel his always high standard.

'I was speaking, just now, when you interrupted me and turned my thoughts to the name Wilberforce, of L. P. Runkle.'

'You said you had an idea he might be going to cooperate.'

'Exactly. Have you ever seen a python after a series of hearty meals?'

'Not to my knowledge.'

'It gets all softened up. It becomes a kindlier, gentler, more lovable python. And if I am not greatly mistaken, the same thing is happening to L. P. Runkle as the result of Anatole's cooking. You saw him at dinner last night.'

'Sorry, no, I wasn't looking. Every fibre of my being was concentrated on the foodstuffs. He would have repaid inspection, would he? Worth seeing, eh?'

'He was positively beaming. He was too busy to utter, but it was plain that he had become all amiability and benevolence. He had the air of a man who would start scattering largesse if given a word of encouragement. It is for Anatole to see to it that this Christmas spirit does not evaporate but comes more and more to the boil. And I know that I can rely on him.'

'Good old Anatole,' I said, lighting a cigarette.

'Amen,' said the ancestor reverently; then, touching on another subject, 'Take that foul cigarette outside, you young hellhound. It smells like an escape of sewer gas.'

Always glad to indulge her lightest whim, I passed through the French window, in a far different mood from that in which I had entered the room. Optimism now reigned in the Wooster bosom. Ginger, I told myself, was going to be all right, Tuppy was going to be all right, and it would not be long before the laughing love god straightened things out between Madeline and Spode, even if he had talked out of turn about stars and daisy chains.

Having finished the gasper, I was about to return and resume conversation with the aged relative, when from within there came the voice of Seppings, now apparently restored to health, and what he was saying froze me in every limb. I couldn't have become stiffer if I had been Lot's wife, whose painful story I had had to read up when I won that Scripture Knowledge prize.

What he was saying ran as follows:

'Mrs McCorkadale, madam.'

Leaning against the side of the house, I breathed rather
in the manner copyrighted by the hart which pants for
cooling streams when heated in the chase. The
realization of how narrowly I had missed having to
mingle again with this blockbusting female barrister
kept me Lot's-wifed for what seemed an hour or so,
though I suppose it can't have been more than a few
seconds. Then gradually I ceased to be a pillar of salt and
was able to concentrate on finding out what on earth Ma
McCorkadale's motive was in paying us this visit. The
last place, I mean to say, where you would have
expected to find her. Considering how she stood in
regard to Ginger, it was as if Napoleon had dropped in
for a chat with Wellington on the eve of Waterloo.

I have had occasion to mention earlier the advantages
as a listening-post afforded by the just-outside-the-
French-window spot where I was standing. Invisible to
those within, I could take in all they were saying, as I
had done with Spode and L. P. Runkle. Both had come
through loud and clear, and neither had had a notion
that Bertram Wooster was on the outskirts, hearing all.

As I could hardly step in and ask her to repeat any of
her remarks which I didn't quite catch, it was fortunate
that the McCorkadale's voice was so robust, while Aunt
Dahlia's, of course, would be audible if you were at Hyde
Park Corner and she in Piccadilly Circus. I have often
thought that the deaf adder I read about when I won my
Scripture Knowledge prize would have got the message
right enough if the aged relative had been one of the
charmers. I was able to continue leaning against the side

of the house in full confidence that I shouldn't miss a syllable of either protagonist's words.

The proceedings started with a couple of Good mornings, Aunt Dahlia's the equivalent of 'What the hell?', and then the McCorkadale, as if aware that it was up to her to offer a word of explanation, said she had called to see Mr Winship on a matter of great importance.

'Is he in?'

Here was a chance for the ancestor to get one up by retorting that he jolly well would be after the votes had been counted, but she let it go, merely saying No, he had gone out, and the McCorkadale said she was sorry.

'I would have preferred to see him in person, but you, I take it, are his hostess, so I can tell you and you will tell him.'

This seemed fair enough to me, and I remember thinking that these barristers put things well, but it appeared to annoy the aged relative.

'I am afraid I do not understand you,' she said, and I knew she was getting steamed up, for if she had been her calm self, she would have said 'Sorry, I don't get you.'

'If you will allow me to explain. I can do so in a few simple words. I have just had a visit from a slimy slinking slug.'

I drew myself up haughtily. Not much good, of course, in the circs, but the gesture seemed called for. One does not object to fair criticism, but this was mere abuse. I could think of nothing in our relations which justified such a description of me. My views on barristers and their way of putting things changed sharply.

Whether or not Aunt Dahlia bridled, as the expression is, I couldn't say, but I think she must have done, for her next words were straight from the deep freeze.

'Are you referring to my nephew Bertram Wooster?'

The McCorkadale did much to remove the bad

impression her previous words had made on me. She said her caller had not given his name, but she was sure he could not have been Mrs Travers's nephew.

'He was a very common man,' she said, and with the quickness which is so characteristic of me I suddenly got on to it that she must be alluding to Bingley, who had been ushered into her presence immediately after I had left. I could understand her applying those derogatory adjectives to Bingley. And the noun slug, just right. Once again I found myself thinking how well barristers put things.

The old ancestor, too, appeared – what's the word beginning with m and meaning less hot under the collar? Mollified, that's it. The suggestion that she could not have a nephew capable of being described as a common man mollified her. I don't say that even now she would have asked Ma McCorkadale to come on a long walking tour with her, but her voice was definitely matier.

'Why do you call him a slug?' she asked, and the McCorkadale had her answer to that.

'For the same reason that I call a spade a spade, because it is the best way of conveying a verbal image of him. He made me a disgraceful proposition.'

'WHAT?' said Aunt Dahlia rather tactlessly.

I could understand her being surprised. It was difficult to envisage a man so eager to collect girl friends as to make disgraceful propositions to Mrs McCorkadale. It amazed me that Bingley could have done it. I had never liked him, but I must confess to a certain admiration for his temerity. Our humble heroes, I felt.

'You're pulling my leg,' said the aged relative.

The McCorkadale came back at her briskly.

'I am doing nothing of the kind. I am telling you precisely what occurred. I was in my drawing-room going over the speech I have prepared for the debate tomorrow, when I was interrupted by the incursion of this man. Naturally annoyed, I asked him what his business was, and he said with a most offensive leer that he was Father Christmas bringing me manna in the wilderness and tidings of great joy. I was about to ring the bell to have him shown out, for of course I assumed that he was intoxicated, when he made me this extraordinary proposition. He had contrived to obtain information to the detriment of my opponent, and this he wished to sell to me. He said it would make my victory in the election certain. It would, as he phrased it, 'be a snip'.

I stirred on my base. If I hadn't been afraid I might be overheard, I would have said 'Aha!' Had circs been other than they were, I would have stepped into the room, tapped the ancestor on the shoulder and said 'Didn't I tell you Bingley had information? Perhaps another time you'll believe me'. But as this would have involved renewing my acquaintance with a woman of whom I had already seen sufficient to last a lifetime, it was not within the sphere of practical politics. I remained, accordingly, where I was, merely hitching my ears up another couple of notches in order not to miss the rest of the dialogue.

After the ancestor had said 'For heaven's sake!' or 'Gorblimey' or whatever it was, indicating that her visitor's story interested her strongly, the McCorkadale resumed. And what she resumed about unquestionably put the frosting on the cake. Words of doom is the only way I can think of to describe the words she spoke as.

'The man, it appeared, was a retired valet, and he belonged to a club for butlers and valets in London, one of the rules of which was that all members were obliged to record in the club book information about their employers. My visitor explained that he had been at one time in the employment of Mr Winship and had duly recorded a number of the latter's escapades which if made public, would be certain to make the worst impression on the voters of Market Snodsbury.'

This surprised me. I hadn't had a notion that Bingley had ever worked for Ginger. It just shows the truth of the old saying that half the world doesn't know how the other three-quarters live.

'He then told me without a blush of shame that on his latest visit to London he had purloined this book and now had it in his possession.'

I gasped with horror. I don't know why, but the thought that Bingley must have been pinching the thing at the very moment when Jeeves and I were sipping our snootfuls in the next room seemed to make it so particularly poignant. Not that it wouldn't have been pretty poignant anyway. For years I had been haunted by the fear that the Junior Ganymede club book, with all the dynamite it contained, would get into the wrong hands, and the hands it had got into couldn't have been more the sort of hands you would have wished it hadn't. I don't know if I make myself clear, but what I'm driving at is that if I had been picking a degraded character to get away with that book, Bingley was the last character I would have picked. I remember Jeeves speaking of someone who was fit for treasons, stratagems and spoils, and that was Bingley all over. The man was wholly without finer feelings, and when you come up against someone without finer feelings, you've had it.

The aged relative was not blind to the drama of the situation. She uttered an awed 'Lord love a duck!', and the McCorkadale said she might well say 'Lord love a duck', though it was not an expression she would have used herself.

'What did you do?' the ancestor asked, all agog, and the McCorkadale gave that sniffing snort of hers. It was partly like an escape of steam and partly like two or three cats unexpectedly encountering two or three dogs, with just a suggestion of a cobra waking up cross in the morning. I wondered how it had affected the late Mr McCorkadale. Probably made him feel that there are worse things than being run over by a municipal tram.

'I sent him away with a flea in his ear. I pride myself on being a fair fighter, and his proposition revolted me. If you want to have him arrested, though I am afraid I cannot see how it can be done, he lives at 5 Ormond Crescent. He appears to have asked my maid to look in and see his etchings on her afternoon off, and he gave her his address. But, as I say, there would seem not to be sufficient evidence for an arrest. Our conversation was without witnesses, and he would simply have to deny possession of the book. A pity. I would have enjoyed seeing a man like that hanged, drawn and quartered.'

She snorted again, and the ancestor, who always knows what the book of etiquette would advise, came across with the soothing syrup. She said Ma McCorkadale deserved a medal.

'Not at all.'

'It was splendid of you to turn the man down.'

'As I said, I am a fair fighter.'

'Apart from your revulsion at his proposition, it must have been very annoying for you to be interrupted when you were working on your speech.'

'Especially as a few moments before this person appeared I had been interrupted by an extraordinary young man who gave me the impression of being half-witted.'

'That would have been my nephew, Bertram Wooster.'

'Oh, I beg your pardon.'

'Quite all right.'

'I may have formed a wrong estimate of his mentality. Our interview was very brief. I just thought it odd that he should be trying to persuade me to vote for my opponent.'

'It's the sort of thing that would seem a bright idea to Bertie. He's like that. Whimsical. Moving in a mysterious way his wonders to perform. But he ought not to have butted in when you were busy with your speech. Is it coming out well?'

'I am satisfied with it.'

'Good for you. I suppose you're looking forward to the debate?'

'Very keenly. I am greatly in favour of it. It simplifies things so much if the two opponents face one another on the same platform and give the voters a chance to compare their views. Provided, of course. that both observe the decencies of debate. But I really must be getting back to my work.'

'Just a moment.' No doubt it was the word 'observe' that had rung a bell with the ancestor. 'Do you do the *Observer* crossword puzzle by any chance?'

'I solve it at breakfast on Sunday mornings.'

'Not the whole lot?'

'Oh yes.'

'Every clue?'

'I have never failed yet. I find it ridiculously simple.'

'Then what's all that song and dance about the measured tread of saints round St Paul's?'

'Oh, I guessed that immediately. The answer, of course, is pedometer. You measure tread with a pedometer. Dome, meaning St Paul's, comes in the middle and Peter, for St Peter, round it. Very simple.'

'Oh, very. Well, thank you. You have taken a great weight off my mind,' said Aunt Dahlia, and they parted in complete amity, a thing I wouldn't have thought possible when Ma McCorkadale was one of the parters.

For perhaps a quarter of a minute after I had rejoined the human herd, as represented by my late father's sister Dahlia, I wasn't able to get a word in, the old ancestor being fully occupied with saying what she thought of the compiler of the *Observer* crossword puzzle, with particular reference to domes and pedometers. And when she had said her say on that subject she embarked on a rueful tribute to the McCorkadale, giving it as her opinion that against a woman with a brain like that Ginger hadn't the meagre chance of a toupee in a high wind. Though, she added in more hopeful vein, now that the menace of the Ganymede Club book had been squashed there was just a possibility that the eloquence of Spode might get his nose in front.

All this while I had been trying to cut in with my opening remark, which was to the effect that the current situation was a bit above the odds, but it was only when I had repeated this for the third time that I succeeded in obtaining her attention.

'This is a bit thick, what,' I said, varying my approach slightly.

She seemed surprised as if the idea had not occurred to her.

'Thick?'

'Well, isn't it?'

'Why? If you were listening, you heard her say that, being a fair fighter, she had scorned the tempter and sent him away with a flea in his ear, which must be a most uncomfortable thing to have. Bingley was baffled.'

'Only for the nonce.'

'Nonsense.'

'Not nonsense, nonce, which isn't at all the same thing. I feel that Bingley, though crushed to earth, will rise again. How about if he sells that book with all its ghastly contents to the *Market Snodsbury Argus-Reminder*?'

I was alluding to the powerful bi-weekly sheet which falls over itself in its efforts to do down the Conservative cause, omitting no word or act to make anyone with Conservative leanings feel like a piece of cheese. Coming out every Wednesday and Saturday with proofs of Ginger's past, I did not see how it could fail to give his candidature the sleeve across the windpipe.

I put this to the old blood relation in no uncertain terms. I might have added that that would wipe the silly smile off her face, but there was no necessity. She saw at once that I spoke sooth, and a crisp hunting-field expletive escaped her. She goggled at me with all the open dismay of an aunt who has inadvertently bitten into a bad oyster.

'I never thought of that!'

'Give it your attention now.'

'Those *Argus-Reminder* hounds stick at nothing.'

'The sky is notoriously their limit.'

'Did you tell me Ginger had done time?'

'I said he was always in the hands of the police on Boat Race night. And, of course, on Rugger night.'

'What's Rugger night?'

'The night of the annual Rugby football encounter between the universities of Oxford and Cambridge. Many blithe spirits get even more effervescent then than when celebrating the Boat Race. Ginger was one of them.'

'He really got jugged?'

'Invariably. His practice of pinching policemen's helmets ensured this. Released next morning on payment of a fine, but definitely after spending the night in a dungeon cell.'

There was no doubt that I had impressed on her the gravity of the situation. She gave a sharp cry like that of a stepped-on dachshund, and her face took on the purple tinge it always assumes in moments of strong emotion.

'This does it!'

'Fairly serious, I agree.'

'Fairly serious! The merest whisper of such goings-on will be enough to alienate every voter in the town. Ginger's done for.'

'You don't think they might excuse him because his blood was young at the time?'

'Not a hope. They won't be worrying about his ruddy blood. You don't know what these blighters here are like. Most of them are chapel folk with a moral code that would have struck Torquemada as too rigid.'

'Torquemada?'

'The Spanish Inquisition man.'

'Oh, that Torquemada.'

'How many Torquemadas did you think there were?'

I admitted that it was not a common name, and she carried on.

'We must act!'

'But how?'

'Or, rather, you must act. You must go to this man and reason with him.'

I h'med a bit at this. I doubted whether a fellow with Bingley's lust for gold would listen to reason.

'What shall I say?'

'You'll know what to say.'

'Oh, shall I?'

'Appeal to his better instincts.'

'He hasn't got any.'

'Now don't make difficulties, Bertie. That's your besetting sin, always arguing. You want to help Ginger, don't you?'

'Of course I do.'

'Very well, then.'

When an aunt has set her mind on a thing, it's no use trying to put in a *nolle prosequi*. I turned to the door.

Half-way there a thought occurred to me. I said:

'How about Jeeves?'

'What about him?'

'We ought to spare his feelings as far as possible. I repeatedly warned him that that club book was high-level explosive and ought not to be in existence. What if it fell into the wrong hands, I said, and he said it couldn't possibly fall into the wrong hands. And now it has fallen into about the wrongest hands it could have fallen into. I haven't the heart to say "I told you so" and watch him writhe with shame and confusion. You see, up till now Jeeves has always been right. His agony on finding that he has at last made a floater will be frightful. I shouldn't wonder if he might not swoon. I can't face him. You'll have to tell him.'

'Yes, I'll do it.'

'Try to break it gently.'

'I will. When you were listening outside, did you get this man Bingley's address?'

'I got it.'

'Then off you go.'

So off I went.

Considering how shaky was his moral outlook and how marked his tendency to weave low plots at the drop of a hat, you would have expected Bingley's headquarters to have been one of those sinister underground dens lit by stumps of candles stuck in the mouths of empty beer bottles such as abound, I believe, in places like Whitechapel and Limehouse. But no. Number 5 Ormond Crescent turned out to be quite an expensive-looking joint with a nice little bit of garden in front of it well supplied with geraniums, bird baths and terracotta gnomes, the sort of establishment that might have belonged to a blameless retired Colonel or a saintly stockbroker. Evidently his late uncle hadn't been just an ordinary small town grocer, weighing out potted meats and raisins to a public that had to watch the pennies, but something on a much more impressive scale. I learned later that he had owned a chain of shops, one of them as far afield as Birmingham, and why the ass had gone and left his money to a chap like Bingley is more than I can tell you, though the probability is that Bingley, before bumping him off with some little-known Asiatic poison, had taken the precaution of forging the will.

On the threshold I paused. I remember in my early days at the private school where I won my Scripture Knowledge prize, Arnold Abney MA, the headmaster, would sometimes announce that he wished to see Wooster in his study after morning prayers, and I always halted at the study door, a prey to uneasiness and apprehension, not liking the shape of things to come. It was much the same now. I shrank from the impending interview. But whereas in the case of A. Abney my disinclination to get things moving had been due to the fear that the proceedings were going to lead up to six of the best from a cane that stung like an adder, with Bingley it was a natural reluctance to ask a favour of a fellow I couldn't stand the sight of. I wouldn't say the Woosters were particularly proud, but we do rather jib at having to grovel to the scum of the earth.

However, it had to be done, and, as I heard Jeeves say once, if it were done, then 'twere well 'twere done quickly. Stiffening the sinews and summoning up the blood, to quote another his gags, I pressed the bell.

If I had any doubts as to Bingley now being in the chips, the sight of the butler who opened the door would have dispelled them. In assembling his domestic staff, Bingley had done himself proud, sparing no expense. I don't say his butler was quite in the class of Jeeves's Uncle Charlie Silversmith, but he came so near it that the breath was taken. And like Uncle Charlie he believed in pomp and ceremony when buttling. I asked him if I could see Mr Bingley, and he said coldly that the master was not receiving.

'I think he'll see me. I'm an old friend of his.'

'I will enquire. Your name, sir?'

'Mr Wooster.'

He pushed off, to return some moments later to say that Mr Bingley would be glad if I would join him in the library. Speaking in what seemed to me a disapproving voice, as though to suggest that, while he was compelled to carry out the master's orders however eccentric, he would never have admitted a chap like me if it had been left to him.

'If you would step this way, sir,' he said haughtily.

What with one thing and another I had rather got out of touch lately with that If-you-would-step-this-way-sir stuff, and it was in a somewhat rattled frame of mind that I entered the library and found Bingley in an armchair with his feet up on an occasional table. He greeted me cordially enough, but with that touch of the patronizing so noticeable at our two previous meetings.

'Ah, Wooster, my dear fellow, come in. I told Bastable to tell everyone I was not at home, but of course you're different. Always glad to see an old pal. And what can I do for you, Wooster?'

I had to say for him that he had made it easy for me to introduce the subject I was anxious to discuss. I was about to get going, when he asked me if I would like a drink. I said No, thanks, and he said in an insufferably smug way that I was probably wise.

'I often thought, when I was staying with you at Chuffnell Regis, that you drank too much, Wooster. Remember how you burned that cottage down? A sober man wouldn't have done that. You must have been stewed to the eyebrows, cocky.'

A hot denial trembled on my lips. I mean to say, it's a bit thick to be chided for burning cottages down by the very chap who put them to the flames. But I restrained myself. The man, I reminded myself, had to be kept in with. If that was how he remembered that night of terror at Chuffnell Regis, it was not for me to destroy his illusions. I refrained from comment, and he asked me if I would like a cigar. When I said I wouldn't, he nodded like a father pleased with a favourite son.

'I am glad to see this improvement in you, Wooster. I always thought you smoked too much. Moderation, moderation in all things, that's the only way. But you were going to tell me why you came here. Just for a chat about old times, was it?'

'It's with ref to that book you pinched from the Junior Ganymede.'

He had been drinking a whisky-and-soda as I spoke, and he drained his glass before replying.

'I wish you wouldn't use that word "pinch",' he said, looking puff-faced. It was plain that I had given offence.

'I simply borrowed it because I needed it in my business. They'll get it back all right.'

'Mrs McCorkadale told my aunt you tried to sell it to her.'

His annoyance increased. His air was that of a man compelled to listen to a tactless oaf who persisted in saying the wrong thing.

'Not sell. I would have had a clause in the agreement saying that she was to return it when she had done with it. The idea I had in mind was that she would have photostatic copies made of the pages dealing with young Winship without the book going out of my possession. But the deal didn't come off. She wouldn't cooperate. Fortunately I have other markets. It's the sort of property there'll be a lot of people bidding for. But why are you so interested, old man? Nothing to do with you, is it?'

'I'm a pal of Ginger Winship's.'

'And I've no objection to him myself. Nice enough young fellow he always seemed to me, though the wrong size.'

'Wrong size?' I said, not getting this.

'His shirts didn't fit me. Not that I hold that against him. These things are all a matter of luck. Don't run away with the idea that I'm a man with a grievance, trying to get back at him for something he did to me when I was staying at his place. Our relations were very pleasant. I quite liked him, and if it didn't matter to me one way or the other who won this election, I'd just as soon he came out on top. But business is business. After studying form I did some pretty heavy betting on McCorkadale, and I've got to protect my investments, old man. That's only common sense, isn't it?'

He paused, apparently expecting a round of applause for his prudence. When I remained *sotto voce* and the silent tomb, he proceeded.

'If you want to get along in this world, Wooster old

chap, you've got to grasp your opportunities. That's what I do. I examine each situation that crops up, and I ask myself "What is there in this for me? How," I ask myself, "can I handle this situation so as to do Rupert Bingley a bit of good?", and it's not often I don't find a way. This time I didn't even have to think. There was young Winship trying to get into Parliament, and here was I standing to win something like a couple of hundred quid if he lost the election, and there was the club book with all the stuff in it which would make it certain he did lose. I recognized it at once as money for jam. The only problem was how to get the book, and I soon solved that. I don't know if you noticed, that day we met at the Junior Ganymede, that I had a large briefcase with me? And that I said I'd got to see the secretary about something? Well, what I wanted to see him about was borrowing the book. And I wouldn't have to find some clever way of getting him looking the other way while I did it, because I knew he'd be out to lunch. So I popped in, popped the book in the briefcase and popped off. Nobody saw me go in. Nobody saw me come out. The whole operation was like taking candy from a kid.'

There are some stories which fill the man of sensibility with horror, repugnance, abhorrence and disgust. I don't mean anecdotes like the one Catsmeat Potter-Pirbright told me at the Drones, I am referring to loathsome revelations such as the bit of autobiography to which I had just been listening. To say that I felt as if the Wooster soul had been spattered with mud by a passing car would not be putting it at all too strongly. I also felt that nothing was to be gained by continuing this distasteful interview. I had had some idea of going into the possibility of Aunt Agatha reading the contents of the club book and touching on the doom, desolation and despair which must inevitably be my portion if she did, but I saw that it would be fruitless or bootless. The

man was without something and pity . . . ruth, would it
be? I know it begins with r . . . and would simply have
given me the horse's laugh. I was now quite certain that
he had murdered his uncle and forged the will. Such a
performance to such a man would have been mere
routine.

I turned, accordingly, to the door, but before I got
there he stopped me, wanting to know if when coming
to stay with Aunt Dahlia I had brought Reggie Jeeves
with me. I said I had, and he said he would like to see
old Reggie again.

'What a cough drop!' he said mirthfully. The word was
strange to me, but weighing it and deciding that it was
intended to be a compliment and a tribute to his many
gifts, I agreed that Jeeves was in the deepest and truest
sense a cough drop.

'Tell Bastable as you go out that if Reggie calls to send
him up. But nobody else.'

'Right ho.'

'Good man, Bastable. He places my bets for me.
Which reminds me. Have you done as I advised and put
a bit on Ma McCorkadale for the Market Snodsbury
stakes? No? Do it without fail, Wooster old man. You'll
never regret it. It'll be like finding money in the street.'

I wasn't feeling any too good as I drove away. I have
described my heart-bowed-down-ness on approaching
the Arnold Abney study door after morning prayers in
the days when I was *in statu pupillari*, as the expression
is, and I was equally apprehensive now as I faced the
prospect of telling the old ancestor of my failure to
deliver the goods in the matter of Bingley. I didn't
suppose that she would give me six of the best, as A.
Abney was so prone to do, but she would certainly not
hesitate to let me know she was displeased. Aunts as a
class are like Napoleon, if it was Napoleon; they expect
their orders to be carried out without a hitch and don't
listen to excuses.

Nor was I mistaken. After lunching at a pub in order to postpone the meeting as long as possible, I returned to the old homestead and made my report, and was unfortunate enough to make it while she was engaged in reading a Rex Stout – in the hard cover, not a paperback. When she threw this at me with the accurate aim which years of practice have given her, its sharp edge took me on the tip of the nose, making me blink not a little.

'I might have known you would mess the whole thing up,' she boomed.

'Not my fault, aged relative,' I said. 'I did my best. Than which,' I added, 'no man can do more.'

I thought I had her there, but I was wrong. It was the sort of line which can generally be counted on to soothe the savage breast, but this time it laid an egg. She snorted. Her snorts are not the sniffing snorts snorted by Ma McCorkadale, they resemble more an explosion in the larger type of ammunition dump and send strong men rocking back on their heels as if struck by lightning.

'How do you mean you did your best? You don't seem to me to have done anything. Did you threaten to have him arrested?'

'No, I didn't do that.'

'Did you grasp him by the throat and shake him like a rat?'

I admitted that that had not occurred to me.

'In other words, you did absolutely nothing,' she said, and thinking it over I had to own that she was perfectly right. It's funny how one doesn't notice these things at the time. It was only now that I realized that I had let Bingley do all the talking, self offering practically nil in the way of a come-back. I could hardly have made less of a contribution to our conversation if I had been the deaf adder I mentioned earlier.

She heaved herself up from the chaise longue on which she was reclining. Her manner was peevish. In time, of course, she would get over her chagrin and start loving her Bertram again as of yore, but there was no getting away from it that an aunt's affection was, as of even date, at its lowest ebb. She said gloomily:

'I'll have to do it myself.'

'Are you going to see Bingley?'

'I am going to see Bingley, and I am going to talk to Bingley, and I am going, if necessary, to take Bingley by the throat and shake him –'

'Like a rat?'

'Yes, like a rat,' she said with the quiet confidence of a woman who had been shaking rats by the throat since she was a slip of a girl. 'Five Ormond Crescent, here I come!'

It shows to what an extent happenings in and about Market Snodsbury had affected my mental processes that she had been gone at least ten minutes before the thought of Bastable floated into my mind, and I wished I had been able to give her a word of warning. That zealous employee of Rupert Bingley had been instructed to see to it that no callers were admitted to the presence, and I saw no reason to suppose that he would fail in his duty when the old ancestor showed up. He would not use physical violence – indeed, with a woman of her physique he would be unwise to attempt it – but it would be the work of an instant with him not to ask her to step this way, thus ensuring her departure with what Ma McCorkadale would call a flea in her ear. I could see her returning in, say, about a quarter of an hour a baffled and defeated woman.

I was right. It was some twenty minutes later, as I sat reading the Rex Stout which she had used as a guided missile, that heavy breathing became audible without and shortly afterwards she became visible within, walking with the measured tread of a saint going round St Paul's. A far less discerning eye than mine could have spotted that she had been having Bastable trouble.

It would have been kinder, perhaps, not to have spoken, but it was one of those occasions when you feel you have to say something.

'Any luck?' I enquired.

She sank on to the chaise longue, simmering gently. She punched a cushion, and I could see she was wishing it could have been Bastable. He was essentially the sort of man who asks, nay clamours, to be treated in this manner.

'No,' she said. 'I couldn't get in.'

'Why was that?' I asked, wearing the mask.

'A beefy butler sort of bird slammed the door in my face.'

'Too bad.'

'And I was just too late to get my foot in.'

'Always necessary to work quick on these occasions. The most precise timing is called for. Odd that he should have admitted me. I suppose my air of quiet distinction was what turned the scale. What did you do?'

'I came away. What else could I have done?'

'No, I can see how difficult it must have been.'

'The maddening part of it is that I was all set to try to get that money out of L. P. Runkle this afternoon. I felt that today was the day. But if my luck's out, as it seems to be, perhaps I had better postpone it.'

'Not strike while the iron is hot?'

'It may not be hot enough.'

'Well, you're the judge. You know,' I said, getting back to the main issue, 'the ambassador to conduct the negotiations with Bingley is really Jeeves. It is he who should have been given the assignment. Where I am speechless in Bingley's presence and you can't even get into the house, he would be inside and talking a blue streak before you could say What ho. And he has the added advantage that Bingley seems fond of him. He thinks he's a cough drop.'

'What on earth's a cough drop?'

'I don't know, but it's something Bingley admires. When he spoke of him as one, it was with a genuine ring of enthusiasm in his voice. Did you tell Jeeves about Bingley having the book?'

'Yes, I told him.'

'How did he take it?'

'You know how Jeeves takes things. One of his eyebrows rose a little and he said he was shocked and astounded.'

'That's strong stuff for him. "Most disturbing" is as far as he goes usually.'

'It's a curious thing,' said the aged relative thoughtfully. 'As I was driving off in the car I thought I saw Jeeves coming away from Bingley's place. Though I couldn't be sure it was him.'

'It must have been. His first move on getting the low-down from you about the book would be to go and see Bingley. I wonder if he's back yet.'

'Not likely. I was driving, he was walking. There wouldn't be time.'

'I'll ring for Seppings and ask. Oh, Seppings,' I said, when he answered the bell, 'Is Jeeves downstairs?'

'No, sir. He went out and has not yet returned.'

'When he does, tell him to come and see me, will you.'

'Very good, sir.'

I thought of asking if Jeeves, when he left, had had the air of a man going to no. 5 Ormond Crescent, but decided that this might be trying Seppings too high, so let it go. He withdrew, and we sat for some time talking about Jeeves. Then, feeling that this wasn't going to get us anywhere and that nothing constructive could be accomplished till he returned, we took up again the matter of L. P. Runkle. At least, the aged relative took it up, and I put the question I had been wanting to put at an earlier stage.

'You say,' I said, 'that you felt today was the day for approaching him. What gave you that idea?'

'The way he tucked into his lunch and the way he talked about it afterwards. Lyrical was the only word for it, and I wasn't surprised. Anatole had surpassed himself.'

'The Suprême de Foie Gras au Champagne?'

'*And* the *Neige aux Perles des Alpes*.'

I heaved a silent sigh, thinking of what might have been. The garbage I had had to insult the Wooster stomach with at the pub had been of a particularly lethal nature. Generally these rural pubs are all right in the matter of browsing, but I had been so unfortunate as to pick one run by a branch of the Borgia family. The thought occurred to me as I ate that if Bingley had given his uncle lunch there one day, he wouldn't have had to go to all the bother and expense of buying little-known Asiatic poisons.

I would have told the old relative this, hoping for sympathy, but at this moment the door opened, and in came Jeeves. Opening the conversation with that gentle cough of his that sounds like a very old sheep clearing its throat on a misty mountain top, he said:

'You wished to see me, sir?'

He couldn't have had a warmer welcome if he had been the prodigal son whose life story I had had to bone up when I won that Scripture Knowledge prize. The welkin, what there was of it in the drawing-room, rang with our excited yappings.

'Come in, Jeeves,' bellowed the aged relative.

'Yes, come in, Jeeves, come in,' I cried. 'We were waiting for you with . . . with what?'

'Bated breath,' said the ancestor.

'That's right. With bated breath and –'

'Tense, quivering nerves. Not to mention twitching muscles and bitten finger nails. Tell me, Jeeves, was that you I saw coming away from 5 Ormond Crescent about an hour ago?'

'Yes, madam.'

'You had been seeing Bingley?'

'Yes, madam.'

'About the book?'

'Yes, madam.'

'Did you tell him he had jolly well got to return it?'

'No, madam.'

'Then why on earth did you go to see him?'

'To obtain the book, madam.'

'But you said you didn't tell him –'

'There was no necessity to broach the subject, madam. He had not yet recovered consciousness. If I might explain. On my arrival at his residence he offered me a drink, which I accepted. He took one himself. We talked for awhile of this and that. Then I succeeded in diverting his attention for a moment, and while his scrutiny was elsewhere I was able to insert a chemical substance in his beverage which had the effect of rendering him temporarily insensible. I thus had ample time to make a search of the room. I had assumed that he would be keeping the book there, and I had not been in error. It was in a lower drawer of the desk. I secured it, and took my departure.'

Stunned by this latest revelation of his efficiency and do-it-yourself-ness, I was unable to utter, but the old ancestor gave the sort of cry or yowl which must have rung over many a hunting field, causing members of the Quorn and the Pytchley to leap in their saddles like Mexican jumping beans.

'You mean you slipped him a Mickey Finn?'

'I believe that is what they are termed in the argot, madam.'

'Do you always carry them about with you?'

'I am seldom without a small supply, madam.'

'Never know when they won't come in handy, eh?'

'Precisely, madam. Opportunities for their use are constantly arising.'

'Well, I can only say thank you. You have snatched victory from the jaws of defeat.'

'It is kind of you to say so, madam.'

'Much obliged, Jeeves.'

'Not at all, madam.'

I was expecting the aged relative to turn to me at this point and tick me off for not having had the sense to give Bingley a Mickey Finn myself, and I knew, for you cannot reason with aunts, that it would be no use pleading that I hadn't got any; but her jocund mood caused her to abstain. Returning to the subject of L. P. Runkle, she said this had made her realize that her luck was in, after all, and she was going to press it.

'I'll go and see him now,' she yipped, 'and I confidently expect to play on him as on a stringed instrument. Out of my way, young Bertie,' she cried, heading for the door, 'or I'll trample you to the dust. Yoicks!' she added, reverting to the patois of the old hunting days. 'Tally ho! Gone away! Hark forrard!'

Or words to that effect.

12

Her departure – at, I should estimate, some sixty m.p.h. – left behind it the sort of quivering stillness you get during hurricane time in America, when the howling gale, having shaken you to the back teeth, passes on to tickle up residents in spots further west. Kind of a dazed feeling it gives you. I turned to Jeeves, and found him, of course, as serene and unmoved as an oyster on the half shell. He might have been watching yowling aunts shoot out of rooms like bullets from early boyhood.

'What was that she said, Jeeves?'

'Yoicks, sir, if I am not mistaken. It seemed to me that Madam also added Tally-ho, Gone away and Hark forrard.'

'I suppose members of the Quorn and the Pytchley are saying that sort of thing all the time.'

'So I understand, sir. It encourages the hounds to renewed efforts. It must, of course, be trying for the fox.'

'I'd hate to be a fox, wouldn't you, Jeeves?'

'Certainly I can imagine more agreeable existences, sir.'

'Not only being chivvied for miles across difficult country but having to listen to men in top hats uttering those uncouth cries.'

'Precisely, sir. A very wearing life.'

I produced my cambric handkerchief and gave the brow a mop. Recent events had caused me to perspire in the manner popularized by the fountains at Versailles.

'Warm work, Jeeves.'

'Yes, sir.'

'Opens the pores a bit.'

'Yes, sir.'

'How quiet everything seems now.'

'Yes, sir. Silence like a poultice comes to heal the blows of sound.'

'Shakespeare?'

'No, sir. The American author Oliver Wendell Holmes. His poem, "The Organ Grinders". An aunt of mine used to read it to me as a child.'

'I didn't know you had any aunts.'

'Three, sir.'

'Are they as jumpy as the one who has just left us?'

'No, sir. Their outlook on life is uniformly placid.'

I had begun to feel a bit more placid myself. Calmer, if you know what I mean. And with the calm had come more charitable thoughts.

'Well, I don't blame the aged relative for being jumpy,' I said. 'She's all tied up with an enterprise of pith and something.'

'Of great pith and moment, sir?'

'That's right.'

'Let us hope that its current will not turn awry and lose the name of action.'

'Yes, let's. Turn what?'

'Awry, sir.'

'Don't you mean agley?'

'No, sir.'

'Then it isn't the poet Burns?'

'No, sir. The words occur in Shakespeare's drama *Hamlet*.'

'Oh, I know *Hamlet*. Aunt Agatha once made me take her son Thos to it at the Old Vic. Not a bad show, I thought, though a bit highbrow. You're sure the poet Burns didn't write it?'

'Yes, sir. The fact, I understand, is well established.'

'Then that settles that. But we have wandered from the point, which is that Aunt Dahlia is up to her neck in this enterprise of great pith and moment. It's about Tuppy Glossop.'

'Indeed, sir?'

'It ought to interest you, because I know you've always liked Tuppy.'

'A very pleasant young gentleman, sir.'

'When he isn't looping back the last ring over the Drones swimming-pool, yes. Well, it's too long a story to tell you at the moment, but the gist of it is this. L. P. Runkle, taking advantage of a legal quibble . . . is it quibble?'

'Yes, sir.'

'Did down Tuppy's father over a business deal . . . no, not exactly a business deal, Tuppy's father was working for him, and he took advantage of the small print in their contract to rob him of the proceeds of something he had invented.'

'It is often the way, sir. The financier is apt to prosper at the expense of the inventor.'

'And Aunt Dahlia is hoping to get him to cough up a bit of cash and slip it to Tuppy.'

'Actuated by remorse, sir?'

'Not just by remorse. She's relying more on the fact that for quite a time he has been under the spell of Anatole's cooking, and she feels that this will have made him a softer and kindlier financier, readier to oblige and do the square thing. You look dubious, Jeeves. Don't you think it will work? She's sure it will.'

'I wish I could share Madam's confidence, but –'

'But, like me, you look on her chance of playing on L. P. Runkle as on a stringed instrument as . . . what? A hundred to eight shot?'

'A somewhat longer price than that, sir. We have to take into consideration the fact that Mr Runkle is . . .'

'Yes? You hesitate, Jeeves, Mr Runkle is what?'

'The expression I am trying to find eludes me, sir. It is one I have sometimes heard you use to indicate a deficiency of sweetness and light in some gentleman of your acquaintance. You have employed it of Mr Spode or, as I should say, Lord Sidcup and, in the days before your association with him took on its present cordiality, of Mr Glossop's uncle, Sir Roderick. It is on the tip of my tongue.'

'A stinker?'

No, he said, it wasn't a stinker.

'A tough baby?'

'No.'

'A twenty-minute egg?'

'That was it, sir. Mr Runkle is a twenty-minute egg.'

'But have you seen enough of him to judge? After all, you've only just met him.'

'Yes, sir, that is true, but Bingley, on learning that he was a guest of Madam's, told me a number of stories illustrative of his hardhearted and implacable character. Bingley was at one time in his employment.'

'Good lord, he seems to have been employed by everyone.'

'Yes, sir, he was inclined to flit. He never remained in one post for long.'

'I don't wonder.'

'But his relationship with Mr Runkle was of more extended duration. He accompanied him to the United States of America some years ago and remained with him for several months.'

'During which period he found him a twenty-minute egg?'

'Precisely, sir. So I very much fear that Madam's efforts will produce no satisfactory results. Would it be a large sum of money that she is hoping to persuade Mr Runkle to part with?'

'Pretty substantial, I gather. You see, what Tuppy's father invented were those Magic Midget things, and Runkle must have made a packet out of them. I suppose she aims at a fifty-fifty split.'

'Then I am forced to the opinion that a hundred to one against is more the figure a level-headed turf accountant would place upon the likelihood of her achieving her objective.'

Not encouraging, you'll agree. In fact, you might describe it as definitely damping. I would have called him a pessimist, only I couldn't think of the word, and while I was trying to hit on something other than 'Gloomy Gus', which would scarcely have been a fitting way to address one of his dignity, Florence came in through the French window and he of course shimmered off. When our conversations are interrupted by the arrival of what you might call the quality, he always disappears like a family spectre vanishing at dawn.

Except at meals I hadn't seen anything of Florence till now, she, so to speak, having taken the high road while I took the low road. What I mean to say is that she was always in Market Snodsbury, bustling about on behalf of the Conservative candidate to whom she was betrothed, while I, after that nerve-racking encounter with the widow of the late McCorkadale, had given up canvassing in favour of curling up with a good book. I had apologized to Ginger for this . . . is pusillanimity the word? . . . and he had taken it extraordinarily well, telling me it was perfectly all right and he wished he could do the same.

She was looking as beautiful as ever, if not more so, and at least ninety-six per cent of the members of the Drones Club would have asked nothing better than to be closeted with her like this. I, however, would willingly have avoided the tête-à-tête, for my trained senses told me that she was in one of her tempers, and when this happens the instinct of all but the hardiest is to climb a tree and pull it up after them. The overbearing dishpotness to which I alluded earlier and which is so marked a feature of her make-up was plainly to the fore. She said, speaking abruptly:

'What are you doing in here on a lovely day like this, Bertie?'

I explained that I had been in conference with Aunt Dahlia, and she riposted that the conference was presumably over by now, Aunt D. being conspicuous by her absence, so why wasn't I out getting fresh air and sunshine.

'You're much too fond of frowsting indoors. That's why you have that sallow look.'

'I didn't know I had a sallow look.'

'Of course you have a sallow look. What else did you expect? You look like the underside of a dead fish.'

My worst fears seemed to be confirmed. I had anticipated that she would work off her choler on the first innocent bystander she met, and it was just my luck that this happened to be me. With bowed head I prepared to face the storm, and then to my surprise she changed the subject.

'I'm looking for Harold,' she said.

'Oh, yes?'

'Have you seen him.'

'I don't think I know him.'

'Don't be a fool. Harold Winship.'

'Oh, Ginger,' I said, enlightened. 'No, he hasn't swum into my ken. What do you want to see him about? Something important?'

'It is important to me, and it ought to be to him. Unless he takes himself in hand, he is going to lose this election.'

'What makes you think that?'

'His behaviour at lunch today.'

'Oh, did he take you to lunch? Where did you go? I had mine at a pub, and the garbage there had to be chewed to be believed. But perhaps you went to a decent hotel?'

'It was the Chamber of Commerce luncheon at the Town Hall. A vitally important occasion, and he made the feeblest speech I have ever heard. A child with water on the brain could have done better. Even you could have done better.'

Well, I suppose placing me on a level of efficiency with a water-on-the-brained child was quite a stately compliment coming from Florence, so I didn't go further into the matter, and she carried on, puffs of flame emerging from both nostrils.

'Er, er, er!'

'I beg your pardon?'

'He kept saying Er. Er, er, er. I could have thrown a coffee spoon at him.'

Here, of course, was my chance to work in the old gag about to err being human, but it didn't seem to me the moment. Instead, I said:

'He was probably nervous.'

'That was his excuse. I told him he had no right to be nervous.'

'Then you've seen him?'

'I saw him.'

'After the lunch?'

'Immediately after the lunch.'

'But you want to see him again?'

'I do.'

'I'll go and look for him, shall I?'

'Yes, and tell him to meet me in Mr Travers's study. We shall not be interrupted there.'

'He's probably sitting in the summerhouse by the lake.'

Well, tell him to stop sitting and come to the study,' she said, for all the world as if she had been Arnold Abney MA announcing that he would like to see Wooster after morning prayers. Quite took me back to the old days.

To get to the summerhouse you have to go across the lawn, the one Spode was toying with the idea of buttering me over, and the first thing I saw as I did so, apart from the birds, bees, butterflies, and what not which put in their leisure hours there, was L. P. Runkle lying in the hammock wrapped in slumber, with Aunt Dahlia in a chair at his side. When she sighted me, she rose, headed in my direction and drew me away a yard or two, at the same time putting a finger to her lips.

'He's asleep,' she said.

A snore from the hammock bore out the truth of this, and I said I could see he was and what a revolting spectacle he presented, and she told me for heaven's sake not to bellow like that. Somewhat piqued at being accused of bellowing by a woman whose lightest whisper was like someone calling the cattle home across the sands of Dee, I said I wasn't bellowing, and she said 'Well, don't.'

'He may be in a nasty mood if he's woken suddenly.'

It was an astute piece of reasoning, speaking well for her grasp of strategy and tactics, but with my quick intelligence I spotted a flaw in it to which I proceeded to call her attention.

'On the other hand, if you don't wake him, how can you plead Tuppy's cause?'

'I said suddenly, ass. It'll be all right if I let Nature take its course.'

'Yes, you may have a point there. Will Nature be long about it, do you think?'

'How do I know?'

'I was only wondering. You can't sit there the rest of the afternoon.'

'I can if necessary.'

'Then I'll leave you to it. I've got to go and look for Ginger. Have you seen him?'

'He came by just now with his secretary on his way to the summerhouse. He told me he had some dictation to do. Why do you want him?'

'I don't particularly, though always glad of his company. Florence told me to find him. She has been giving him hell and is anxious to give him some more. Apparently –'

Here she interrupted me with a sharp 'Hist!', for L. P. Runkle had stirred in his sleep and it looked as if life was returning to the inert frame. But it proved to be a false alarm, and I resumed my remarks.

'Apparently he failed to wow the customers at the Chamber of Commerce lunch, where she had been counting on him being a regular . . . who was the Greek chap?'

'Bertie, if I wasn't afraid of waking Runkle, I'd strike you with a blunt instrument, if I had a blunt instrument. What Greek chap?'

'That's what I'm asking you. He chewed pebbles.'

'Do you mean Demosthenes?'

'You may be right. I'll take it up later with Jeeves. Florence was expecting Ginger to be a regular Demosthenes, if that was the name, which seems unlikely, though I was at school with a fellow called Gianbattista, and he let her down, and this has annoyed her. You know how she speaks her mind, when annoyed.'

'She speaks her mind much too much,' said the relative severely. 'I wonder Ginger stands it.'

It so happened that I was in a position to solve the problem that was perplexing her. The facts governing the relationship of guys and dolls had long been an open book to me. I had given deep thought to the matter, and when I give deep thought to a matter perplexities are speedily ironed out.

'He stands it, aged relative, because he loves her, and you wouldn't be far wrong in saying that love conquers all. I know what you mean, of course. It surprises you that a fellow of his thews and sinews should curl up in a ball when she looks squiggle-eyed at him and receive her strictures, if that's the word I want, with the meekness of a spaniel rebuked for bringing a decaying bone into the drawing-room. What you overlook is the fact that in the matter of finely chiselled profile, willowy figure and platinum-blonde hair she is well up among the top ten, and these things weigh with a man like Ginger. You and I, regarding Florence coolly, pencil her in as too bossy for human consumption, but he gets a different slant. It's the old business of what Jeeves calls the psychology of the individual. Very possibly the seeds of rebellion start to seethe within him when she speaks her mind, but he catches sight of her sideways or gets a glimpse of her hair, assuming for purposes of argument that she isn't wearing a hat, or notices once again that she has as many curves as a scenic railway, and he feels that it's worth putting up with a spot of mind-speaking in order to make her his own. His love, you see, is not wholly spiritual. There's a bit of the carnal mixed up in it.'

I would have spoken further, for the subject was one that always calls out the best in me, but at this point the old ancestor, who had been fidgeting for some time, asked me to go and drown myself in the lake. I buzzed off, accordingly, and she returned to her chair beside the hammock, brooding over L. P. Runkle like a mother over her sleeping child.

I don't suppose she had observed it, for aunts seldom give much attention to the play of expression on the faces of their nephews, but all through these exchanges I had been looking grave, making it pretty obvious that there was something on my mind. I was thinking of what Jeeves had said about the hundred to one which a level-headed bookie would wager against her chance of extracting money from a man so liberally equipped with one-way pockets as L. P. Runkle, and it pained me deeply to picture her dismay and disappointment when, waking from his slumbers, he refused to disgorge. It would be a blow calculated to take all the stuffing out of her, she having been so convinced that she was on a sure thing.

I was also, of course, greatly concerned about Ginger. Having been engaged to Florence myself, I knew what she could do in the way of ticking off the errant male, and the symptoms seemed to point to the probability that on the present occasion she would eclipse all previous performances. I had not failed to interpret the significance of that dark frown, that bitten lip and those flashing eyes, nor the way the willowy figure had quivered, indicating, unless she had caught a chill, that she was as sore as a sunburned neck. I marvelled at the depths to which my old friend must have sunk as an orator in order to get such stark emotions under way, and I intended – delicately, of course – to question him about this.

I had, however, no opportunity to do so, for on entering the summerhouse the first thing I saw was him and Magnolia Glendennon locked in an embrace so close that it seemed to me that only powerful machinery could unglue them.

13

In taking this view, however, I was in error, for scarcely
had I uttered the first yip of astonishment when the
Glendennon popsy, echoing it with a yip of her own
such as might have proceeded from a nymph surprised
while bathing, disentangled herself and came whizzing
past me, disappearing into the great world outside at a
speed which put her in the old ancestor's class as a
sprinter on the flat. It was as though she had said 'Oh for
the wings of a dove' and had got them.

I, meanwhile, stood rooted to the s., the mouth
slightly ajar and the eyes bulging to their fullest extent.
What's that word beginning with dis? Disembodied? No,
not disembodied. Distemper? No, not distemper.
Disconcerted, that's the one. I was disconcerted. I should
imagine that if you happened to wander by accident into
the steam room of a Turkish bath on Ladies' Night, you
would have emotions very similar to those I was
experiencing now.

Ginger, too, seemed not altogether at his ease. Indeed,
I would describe him as definitely taken aback. He
breathed heavily, as if suffering from asthma; the eye
with which he regarded me contained practically none of
the chumminess you would expect to see in the eye of
an old friend; and his voice, when he spoke, resembled
that of an annoyed cinnamon bear. Throaty, if you know
what I mean, and on the peevish side. His opening words
consisted of a well-phrased critique of my tactlessness in
selecting that particular moment for entering the
summerhouse. He wished, he said, that I wouldn't creep
about like a ruddy detective. Had I, he asked, got my

magnifying glass with me and did I propose to go around on all fours, picking up small objects and putting them away carefully in an envelope? What, he enquired, was I doing here, anyway?

To this I might have replied that I was perfectly entitled at all times to enter a summerhouse which was the property of my Aunt Dahlia and so related to me by ties of blood, but something told me that suavity would be the better policy. In rebuttal, therefore, I merely said that I wasn't creeping about like a ruddy detective, but navigating with a firm and manly stride, and had simply been looking for him because Florence had ordered me to and I had learned from a usually well-informed source that this was where he was.

My reasoning had the soothing effect I had hoped for. His manner changed, losing its cinnamon bear quality and taking on a welcome all-pals-together-ness. It bore out what I have always said, that there's nothing like suavity for pouring oil on the troubled w.'s. When he spoke again, it was plain that he regarded me as a friend and an ally.

'I suppose all this seems a bit odd to you, Bertie.'

'Not at all, old man, not at all.'

'But there is a simple explanation. I love Magnolia.'

'I thought you loved Florence.'

'So did I. But you know how apt one is to make mistakes.'

'Of course.'

'When you're looking for the ideal girl, I mean.'

'Quite.'

'I dare say you've had the same experience yourself.'

'From time to time.'

'Happens to everybody, I expect.'

'I shouldn't wonder.'

'Where one goes wrong when looking for the ideal girl is in making one's selection before walking the full length of the counter. You meet someone with a perfect

profile, platinum-blonde hair and a willowy figure, and
you think your search is over. "Bingo!" you say to
yourself. "This is the one. Accept no substitutes." Little
knowing that you are linking your lot with that of a
female sergeant-major with strong views on the subject
of discipline, and that if you'd only gone on a bit further
you would have found the sweetest, kindest, gentlest
girl that ever took down outgoing mail in shorthand,
who would love you and cherish you and would never
dream of giving you hell, no matter what the
circumstances. I allude to Magnolia Glendennon.'

'I thought you did.'

'I can't tell you how I feel about her, Bertie.'

'Don't try.'

'Ever since we came down here I've had a lurking
suspicion that she was the mate for me and that in
signing on the dotted line with Florence I had made the
boner of a lifetime. Just now my last doubts were
dispelled.'

'What happened just now?'

'She rubbed the back of my neck. My interview with
Florence, coming on top of that ghastly Chamber of
Commerce lunch, had given me a splitting headache,
and she rubbed the back of my neck. Then I knew. As
those soft fingers touched my skin like dainty butterflies
hovering over a flower –'

'Right-ho.'

'It was a revelation, Bertie. I knew that I had come to
journey's end. I said to myself, "This is a good thing.
Push it along." I turned. I grasped her hand. I gazed into
her eyes. She gazed into mine. I told her I loved her. She
said so she did me. She fell into my arms. I grabbed her.
We stood murmuring endearments, and for a while
everything was fine. Couldn't have been better. Then a
thought struck me. There was a snag. You've probably
spotted it.'

'Florence?'

'Exactly. Bossy though she is, plain-spoken though she may be when anything displeases her, and I wish you could have heard her after that Chamber of Commerce lunch, I am still engaged to her. And while girls can break engagements till the cows come home, men can't.'

I followed his train of thought. It was evident that he, like me, aimed at being a *preux chevalier*, and you simply can't be *preux* or anything like it if you go about the place getting betrothed and then telling the party of the second part it's all off. It seemed to me that the snag which had raised its ugly head was one of formidable – you might say king-size – dimensions, well calculated to make the current of whatever he proposed to do about it turn awry and lose the name of action. But when I put this to him with a sympathetic tremor in my voice, and I'm not sure I didn't clasp his hand, he surprised me by chuckling like a leaky radiator.

'That's all right,' he said. 'It would, I admit, appear to be a tricky situation, but I can handle it. I'm going to get Florence to break the engagement.'

He spoke with such a gay, confident ring in his voice, so like the old ancestor predicting what she was going to do to L.P. Runkle in the playing-on-a-stringed-instrument line, that I was loath, if that's the word I want, to say anything to depress him, but the question had to be asked.

'How?' I said, asking it.

'Quite simple. We agreed, I think, that she has no use for a loser. I propose to lose this election.'

Well, it was a thought of course, and I was in complete agreement with his supposition that if the McCorkadale nosed ahead of him in the voting, Florence would in all probability hand him the pink slip, but where it seemed to me that the current went awry was that he had no means of knowing that the electorate would put him in second place. Of course voters are like aunts, you never know what they will be up to from one day to the next, but it was a thing you couldn't count on.

I mentioned this to him, and he repeated his impersonation of a leaky radiator.

'Don't you worry, Bertie. I have the situation well in hand. Something happened in a dark corner of the Town Hall after lunch which justifies my confidence.'

'What happened in a dark corner of the Town Hall after lunch?'

'Well, the first thing that happened after lunch was that Florence got hold of me and became extremely personal. It was then that I realized that it would be the act of a fathead to marry her.'

I nodded adhesion to this sentiment. That time when she had broken her engagement with me my spirits had soared and I had gone about singing like a relieved nightingale.

One thing rather puzzled me and seemed to call for explanatory notes.

'Why did Florence draw you into a dark corner when planning to become personal?' I asked. 'I wouldn't have credited her with so much tact and consideration. As a rule, when she's telling people what she thinks of them, an audience seems to stimulate her. I recall one occasion when she ticked me off in the presence of seventeen Girl Guides, all listening with their ears flapping, and she had never spoken more fluently.'

He put me straight on the point I had raised. He said he had misled me.

'It wasn't Florence who drew me into the dark corner, it was Bingley.'

'Bingley?'

'A fellow who worked for me once.'

'He worked for me once.'

'Really? It's a small world, isn't it.'

'Pretty small. Did you know he'd come into money?'

'He'll soon be coming into some more.'

'But you were saying he drew you into the dark corner. Why did he do that?'

'Because he had a proposition to make to me which demanded privacy. He . . . but before going on I must lay a proper foundation. You know in those Perry Mason stories how whenever Perry says anything while cross-examining a witness, the District Attorney jumps up and yells "Objection, your honour. The SOB has laid no proper foundation". Well, then, you must know that this man Bingley belongs to a butlers and valets club in London called the Junior Ganymede, and one of the rules there is that members have to record the doings of their employers in the club book.'

I would have told him I knew all too well about that, but he carried on before I could speak.

'Such a book, as you can imagine, contains a lot of damaging stuff, and he told me he had been obliged to contribute several pages about me which, if revealed, would lose me so many votes that the election would be a gift to my opponent. He added that some men in his place would have sold it to the opposition and made a lot of money, but he wouldn't do a thing like that because it would be low and in the short time we were together he had come to have a great affection for me. I had never realized before what an extraordinarily good chap he was. I had always thought him a bit of a squirt. Shows how wrong you can be about people.'

Again I would have spoken, but he rolled over me like a tidal wave.

'I should have explained that the committee of the Junior Ganymede, recognizing the importance of this book, had entrusted it to him with instructions to guard it with his life, and his constant fear was that bad men would get wind of this and try to steal it. So what would remove a great burden from his mind, he said, would be if I took it into my possession. Then I could be sure that its contents wouldn't be used against me. I could return

it to him after the election and slip him a few quid, if I
wished, as a token of my gratitude. You can picture me
smiling my subtle smile as he said this. He little knew
that my first act would be to send the thing by
messenger to the offices of the *Market Snodsbury
Argus-Reminder*, thereby handing the election on a plate
to the McCorkadale and enabling me to free myself from
my honourable obligations to Florence, who would of
course, on reading the stuff, recoil from me in horror. Do
you know the *Argus-Reminder*? Very far to the left.
Can't stand Conservatives. It had a cartoon of me last
week showing me with my hands dripping with the
blood of the martyred proletariat. I don't know where
they get these ideas. I've never spilled a drop of
anybody's blood except when boxing, and then the other
chap was spilling mine – wholesome give and take. So it
wasn't long before Bingley and I had everything all fixed
up. He couldn't give me the book then, as he had left it
at home, and he wouldn't come and have a drink with
me because he had to hurry back because he thought
Jeeves might be calling and he didn't want to miss him.
Apparently Jeeves is a pal of his – old club crony, that
sort of thing. We're meeting tomorrow. I shall reward
him with a purse of gold, he will give me the book, and
five minutes later, if I can find some brown paper and
string, it will be on its way to the *Argus-Reminder*. The
material should be in print the day after tomorrow.
Allow an hour or so for Florence to get hold of a copy
and say twenty minutes for a chat with her after she's
read it, and I ought to be a free man well before lunch.
About how much gold do you think I should reward
Bingley with? Figures were not named, but I thought at
least a hundred quid, because he certainly deserves
something substantial for his scrupulous
high-mindedness. As he said, some men in his place
would have sold the book to the opposition and cleaned
up big.'

By what I have always thought an odd coincidence he paused at this point and asked me why I was looking like something the cat brought in, precisely as the aged relative had asked me after my interview with Ma McCorkadale. I don't know what cats bring into houses, but one assumes that it is something not very jaunty, and apparently, when in the grip of any strong emotion, I resemble their treasure trove. I could well understand that I was looking like that now. I find it distasteful to have to shatter a long-time buddy's hopes and dreams, and no doubt this shows on the surface.

There was no sense in beating about bushes. It was another of those cases of if it were done, then 'twere well 'twere done quickly.

'Ginger,' I said, 'I'm afraid I have a bit of bad news for you. That book is no longer among those present. Jeeves called on Bingley, gave him a Mickey Finn and got it away from him. He now has it among his archives.'

He didn't get it at first, and I had to explain.

'Bingley is not the man of integrity you think him. He is on the contrary a louse of the first water. You might describe him as a slimy slinking slug. He pinched that book from the Junior Ganymede and tried to sell it to the McCorkadale. She sent him away with a flea in his ear because she was a fair fighter, and he tried to sell it to you. But meanwhile Jeeves nipped in and obtained it.'

It took him perhaps a minute to absorb this, but to my surprise he wasn't a bit upset.

'Well, that's all right. Jeeves can take it to the *Argus-Reminder*.'

I shook the loaf sadly, for I knew that this time those hopes and dreams of his were really due for a sock in the eye.

'He wouldn't do it, Ginger. To Jeeves that club book is sacred. I've gone after him a dozen times, urging him to destroy the pages concerning me, but he always remains as unco-operative as Balaam's ass, who, you may

remember, dug his feet in and firmly refused to play ball.
He'll never let it out of his hands.'

He took it, as I had foreseen, big. He spluttered a good
deal. He also kicked the table and would have splintered
it if it hadn't been made of marble. It must have hurt
like sin, but what disturbed him, I deduced, was not so
much the pain of a bruised toe as spiritual anguish. His
eyes glittered, his nose wiggled, and if he was not
gnashing his teeth I don't know a gnashed tooth when I
hear one.

'Oh, won't he?' he said, going back into the old
cinnamon bear routine. 'He won't, won't he? We'll see
about that. Pop off, Bertie. I want to think.'

I popped off, glad to do so. These displays of naked
emotion take it out of one.

14

The shortest way to the house was across the lawn, but I didn't take it. Instead, I made for the back door. It was imperative, I felt, that I should see Jeeves without delay and tell him of the passions he had unchained and warn him, until the hot blood had had time to cool, to keep out of Ginger's way. I hadn't at all liked the sound of the latter's 'We'll see about that', nor the clashing of those gnashed teeth. I didn't of course suppose that, however much on the boil, he would inflict personal violence on Jeeves – sock him, if you prefer the expression – but he would certainly say things to him which would wound his feelings and cause their relations, so pleasant up to now, to deteriorate. And naturally I didn't want that to happen.

Jeeves was in a deck-chair outside the back door, reading Spinoza with the cat Augustus on his lap. I had given him the Spinoza at Christmas and he was constantly immersed in it. I hadn't dipped into it myself, but he tells me it is good ripe stuff, well worth perusal.

He would have risen at my approach, but I begged him to remain seated, for I knew that Augustus, like L. P. Runkle, resented being woken suddenly, and one always wants to consider a cat's feelings.

'Jeeves,' I said, 'a somewhat peculiar situation has popped up out of a trap, and I would be happy to have your comments on it. I am sorry to butt in when you are absorbed in your Spinoza and have probably just got to the part where the second corpse is discovered, but what I have to say is of great pith and moment, so listen attentively.'

'Very good, sir.'

'The facts are these,' I said, and without further preamble or whatever they call it I embarked on my narrative. 'Such,' I concluded some minutes later, 'is the position of affairs, and I think you will agree that the problem confronting us presents certain points of interest.'

'Undeniably, sir.'

'Somehow Ginger has got to lose the election.'

'Precisely, sir.'

'But how?'

'It is difficult to say on the spur of the moment, sir. The tide of popular opinion appears to be swaying in Mr Winship's direction. Lord Sidcup's eloquence is having a marked effect on the electorate and may well prove the deciding factor. Mr Seppings, who obliged as an extra waiter at the luncheon, reports that his lordship's address to the members of the Market Snodsbury Chamber of Commerce was sensational in its brilliance. He tells me that, owing entirely to his lordship, the odds to be obtained in the various public houses, which at one time favoured Mrs McCorkadale at ten to six, have now sunk to evens.'

'I don't like that, Jeeves.'

'No, sir, it is ominous.'

'Of course, if you were to release the club book . . .'

'I fear I cannot do that, sir.'

'No, I told Ginger you regarded it as a sacred trust. Then nothing can be done except to urge you to get the old brain working.'

'I will certainly do my utmost, sir.'

'No doubt something will eventually emerge. Keep eating lots of fish. And meanwhile stay away from Ginger as much as possible, for he is in ugly mood.'

'I quite understand, sir. Stockish, hard and full of rage.'

'Shakespeare?'

'Yes, sir. His *merchant of Venice*.'

I left him then, pleased at having got one right for a change, and headed for the drawing-room, hoping for another quiet go at the Rex Stout which the swirling rush of events had forced me to abandon. I was, however, too late. The old ancestor was on the chaise longue with it in her grasp, and I knew that I had small chance of wresting it from her. No one who has got his or her hooks on a Rex Stout lightly lets it go.

Her presence there surprised me. I had supposed that she was still brooding over the hammock and its contents.

'Hullo,' I said, 'have you finished with Runkle?'

She looked up, and I noted a trace of annoyance in her demeanour. I assumed that Nero Wolfe had come down from the orchid room and told Archie Goodwin to phone Saul Panzer and Orrie what's his name and things were starting to warm up. In which event she would naturally resent the intrusion of even a loved nephew whom she had often dandled on her knee – not recently, I don't mean, but when I was a bit younger.

'Oh, it's you,' she said, which it was of course. 'No, I haven't finished with Runkle. I haven't even begun. He's still asleep.'

She gave me the impression of being not much in the mood for chit-chat, but one has to say something on these occasions. I brought up a subject which I felt presented certain points of interest.

'Have you ever noticed the remarkable resemblance between L. P. Runkle's daily habits and those of the cat Augustus? They seem to spend all their time sleeping. Do you think they've got traumatic symplegia?'

'What on earth's that?'

'I happened to come on it in a medical book I was reading. It's a disease that makes you sleep all the time. Has Runkle shown no signs of waking?'

'Yes, he did, and just as he was beginning to stir Madeline Bassett came along. She said could she speak to me, so I had to let her. It wasn't easy to follow what she was saying, because she was sobbing all the time, but I got it at last. It was all about the rift with Spode. I told you they had had a tiff. It turns out to be more serious than that. You remember me telling you he couldn't be a Member of Parliament because he was a peer. Well, he wants to give up his title so that he will be eligible.'

'Can a fellow with a title give it up? I thought he was stuck with it.'

'He couldn't at one time, at least only by being guilty of treason, but they've changed the rules and apparently it's quite the posh thing to do nowadays.'

'Sounds silly.'

'That's the view Madeline takes.'

'Did she say what put the idea into Spode's fat head?'

'No, but I can see what did. He has made such a smash hit with his speeches down here that he's saying to himself "Why am I sweating like this on behalf of somebody else? Why not go into business for myself?" Who was it said someone was intoxicated with the exuberance of his own verbosity?'

'I don't know.'

'Jeeves would. It was Bernard Shaw or Mark Twain or Jack Dempsey or somebody. Anyway, that's Spode. He's all puffed up and feels he needs a wider scope. He sees himself holding the House of Commons spellbound.'

'Why can't he hold the House of Lords spellbound?'

'It wouldn't be the same thing. It would be like playing in the Market Snodsbury tennis tournament instead of electrifying one and all on the centre court at Wimbledon. I can see his point.'

'I can't.'

'Nor can Madeline. She's all worked up about it, and I can understand how she feels. No joke for a girl who thinks she's going to be the Countess of Sidcup to have the fellow say "April fool, my little chickadee. What you're going to be is Mrs Spode." If I had been told at Madeline's age that Tom had been made a peer and I then learned that he was going to back out of it and I wouldn't be able to call myself Lady Market Snodsbury after all, I'd have kicked like a mule. Titles to a girl are like catnip to a cat.'

'Can nothing be done?'

'The best plan would be for you to go to him and tell him how much we all admire him for being Lord Sidcup and what a pity it would be for him to go back to a ghastly name like Spode.'

'What's the next best plan?'

'Ah, that wants thinking out.'

We fell into a thoughtful silence, on my part an uneasy one. I didn't at this juncture fully appreciate the peril that lurked, but anything in the nature of a rift within the lute between Spode and Madeline was always calculated to make me purse the lips to some extent. I was still trying to hit on some plan which would be more to my taste than telling Spode what a pity it would be for him to stop being the Earl of Sidcup and go back to a ghastly name like his, when my reverie was broken by the entry through the French window of the cat Augustus, for once awake and in full possession of his faculties, such as they were. No doubt in a misty dreamlike sort of way he had seen me when I was talking to Jeeves and had followed me on my departure, feeling, after those breakfasts of ours together, that association with me was pretty well bound to culminate in kippers. A vain hope, of course. The well-dressed man does not go around with kippered herrings in his pocket. But one of the lessons life teaches us is that cats will be cats.

As is my unvarying policy when closeted with one of these fauna, I made chirruping noises and bent down to tickle the back of the dumb chum's left ear, but my heart was not in the tickling. The more I mused on the recent conversation, the less I liked what the aged relative had revealed. Telling Augustus that I would be back with him in a moment, I straightened myself and was about to ask her for further details, when I discovered that she was no longer in my midst. She must suddenly have decided to have another pop at L. P. Runkle and was presumably even now putting Tuppy's case before him. Well, best of luck to her, of course, and nice to think she had a fine day for it, but I regretted her absence. When your mind is weighed down with matters of great pith and moment, it gives you a sort of sinking feeling to be alone. No doubt the boy who stood on the burning deck whence all but he had fled had this experience.

However, I wasn't alone for long. Scarcely had Augustus sprung on to my lap and started catching up with his sleep when the door opened and Spode came in.

I leaped to my feet, causing Augustus to fall to earth I knew not where, as the fellow said. I was a prey to the liveliest apprehensions. My relations with Spode had been for long so consistently strained that I never saw him nowadays without a lurking fear that he was going to sock me in the eye. Obviously I wasn't to be blamed if he and Madeline had been having trouble, but that wouldn't stop him blaming me. It was like the story of the chap who was in prison and a friend calls and asks him why and the chap tells him and the friend says But they can't put you in prison for that and the chap says I know they can't, but they have. Spode didn't have to have logical reasons for setting about people he wasn't fond of, and it might be that he was like Florence and would work off his grouch on the first available innocent bystander. Putting it in a nutshell, my frame of mind was approximately that of the fellows in the hymn who got such a start when they looked over their shoulders and saw the troops of Midian prowling and prowling around.

It was with profound relief, therefore, that I suddenly
got on to it that his demeanour was free from hostility.
He was looking like somebody who has just seen the
horse on which he had put all his savings, plus whatever
he had been able to lift from his employer's till, beaten
by a short head. His face, nothing to write home about at
the best of times, was drawn and contorted, but with
pain rather than the urge to commit mayhem. And
while one would always prefer him not to be present, a
drawn-and-contorted-with-pain Spode was certainly the
next best thing. My greeting, in consequence, had the
real ring of cordiality in it.

'Oh, hullo, Spode, hullo. There you are, what?
Splendid.'

'Can I have a word with you, Wooster?'

'Of course, of course. Have several.'

He did not speak for a minute or so, filling in the
time by subjecting me to a close scrutiny. Then he gave
a sigh and shook his head.

'I can't understand it,' he said.

'What can't you understand, Spode old man or rather
Lord Sidcup old man?' I asked in a kind voice, for I was
only too willing to help this new and improved Spode
solve any little problem that was puzzling him.

'How Madeline can contemplate marrying a man like
you. She has broken our engagement and says that's
what she's going to do. She was quite definite about it.
"All is over," she said. "Here is your ring," she said. "I
shall marry Bertie Wooster and make him happy," she
said. You can't want it plainer than that.'

I stiffened from head to f. Even with conditions what
they were in this disturbed post-war world I hadn't been
expecting to be turned into a pillar of salt again for some
considerable time, but this had done it. I don't know
how many of my public have ever been slapped between
the eyes with a wet fish, but those who have will
appreciate my emotions as the seventh Earl of Sidcup

delivered this devastating bulletin. Everything started to go all wobbly, and through what is known as a murky mist I seemed to be watching a quivering-at-the-edges seventh Earl performing the sort of gyrations travelled friends have told me the Ouled Nail dancers do in Cairo.

I was stunned. It seemed to me incredible that Madeline Bassett should have blown the whistle on their engagement. Then I remembered that at the time when she had plighted her troth Spode was dangling a countess's coronet before her eyes, and the thing became more understandable. I mean, take away the coronet and what had you got? Just Spode. Not good enough, a girl would naturally feel.

He, meanwhile, was going on to explain why he found it so bizarre that Madeline should be contemplating marrying me, and almost immediately I saw that I had been mistaken in supposing that he was not hostile. He spoke from between clenched teeth, and that always tells the story.

'As far as I can see, Wooster, you are without attraction of any kind. Intelligence? No. Looks? No. Efficiency? No. You can't even steal an umbrella without getting caught. All that can be said for you is that you don't wear a moustache. They tell me you did grow one once, but mercifully shaved it off. That is to your credit, but it is a small thing to weigh in the balance against all your other defects. When one considers how numerous these are, one can only suppose that it is your shady record of stealing anything you can lay your hands on that appeals to Madeline's romantic soul. She is marrying you in the hope of reforming you, and let me tell you, Wooster, that if you disappoint that hope, you will be sorry. She may have rejected me, but I shall always love her as I have done since she was so high, and I shall do my utmost to see that her gentle heart is not broken by any sneaking son of a what not who looks like a chorus boy in a touring revue playing

the small towns and cannot see anything of value
without pocketing it. You will probably think you are
safe from me when you are doing your stretch in
Wormwood Scrubs for larceny, but I shall be waiting for
you when you come out and I shall tear you limb from
limb. And,' he added, for his was a one-track mind,
'dance on the fragments in hobnailed boots.'

He paused, produced his cigarette case, asked me if I
had a match, thanked me when I gave him one, and
withdrew.

He left behind him a Bertram Wooster whom the
dullest eye could have spotted as not being at the peak of
his form. The prospect of being linked for life to a girl
who would come down to breakfast and put her hands
over my eyes and say 'Guess who' had given my morale
a sickening wallop, reducing me to the level of one of
those wee sleekit timorous cowering beasties Jeeves tells
me the poet Burns used to write about. It is always my
policy in times of crisis to try to look on the bright side,
but I make one proviso – viz. that there has to be a
bright side to look on, and in the present case there
wasn't even the sniff of one.

As I sat there draining the bitter cup, there were
noises off stage and my meditations were interrupted by
the return of the old ancestor. Well, when I say return,
she came whizzing in but didn't stop, just whizzed
through, and I saw, for I am pretty quick at noticing
things, that she was upset about something. Reasoning
closely, I deduced that her interview with L. P. Runkle
must have gone awry or, as I much prefer to put it, agley.

And so it proved when she bobbed up again some little
time later. Her first observation was that L. P. Runkle
was an illegitimate offspring to end all illegitimate
offsprings, and I hastened to commiserate with her. I
could have done with a bit of commiseration myself, but
Women and Children First is always the Wooster slogan.

'No luck?' I said.

'None.'

'Wouldn't part?'

'Not a penny.'

'You mentioned that without his co-operation Tuppy and Angela's wedding bells would not ring out?'

'Of course I did. And he said it was a great mistake for young people to marry before they knew their own minds.'

'You could have pointed out that Tuppy and Angela have been engaged for two years.'

'I did.'

'What did he say to that?'

'He said "Not nearly long enough".'

'So what are you going to do?'

'I've done it,' said the old ancestor. 'I pinched his porringer.'

15

I goggled at her, one hundred per cent non-plussed. She had spoken with the exuberance of an aunt busily engaged in patting herself between the shoulder-blades for having done something particularly clever, but I could make nothing of her statement. This habit of speaking in riddles seemed to be growing on her.

'You what?' I said. 'You pinched his what?'

'His porringer. I told you about it the day you got here. Don't you remember? That silver thing he came to try to sell to Tom.'

She had refreshed my memory. I recalled the conversation to which she referred. I had asked her why she was entertaining in her home a waste product like L. P. Runkle, and she had said that he had come hoping to sell Uncle Tom a silver something for his collection and she had got him to stay on in order to soften him up with Anatole's cooking and put to him, when softened up, her request for cash for Tuppy.

'When he turned me down just now, it suddenly occurred to me that if I got hold of the thing and told him he wouldn't get it back unless he made a satisfactory settlement, I would have a valuable bargaining point and we could discuss the matter further at any time that suited him.'

I was ap-what-is-it. Forget my own name next. Appalled, that's the word, though shocked to the core would be about as good; nothing much in it, really. I hadn't read any of those etiquette books you see all over the place, but I was prepared to bet that the leaders of Society who wrote them would raise an eyebrow or two at carrying-ons of this description. The chapter on Hints To Hostesses would be bound to have a couple of paragraphs warning them that it wasn't the done thing to invite people to the home and having got them settled in to pinch their porringers.

'But good Lord!' I ejaculated, appalled or, if you prefer it, shocked to the core.

'Now what?'

'The man is under your roof.'

'Did you expect him to be on it?'

'He has eaten your salt.'

'Very imprudent, with blood pressure like his. His doctor probably forbids it.'

'You can't do this.'

'I know I can't, but I have,' she said, just like the chap in the story, and I saw it would be fruitless or bootless to go on arguing. It rarely is with aunts – if you're their nephew, I mean, because they were at your side all through your formative years and know what an ass you were then and can't believe that anything that you may say later is worth listening to. I shouldn't be at all surprised if Jeeves's three aunts don't shut him up when he starts talking, remembering that at the age of six the child Jeeves didn't know the difference between the poet Burns and a hole in the ground.

Ceasing to expostulate, therefore, if expostulate is the word I want, I went to the bell and pressed it, and when she asked for footnotes throwing a light on why I did this, I told her I proposed to place the matter in the hands of a higher power.

'I'm ringing for Jeeves.'

'You'll only get Seppings.'

'Seppings will provide Jeeves.'

'And what do you think Jeeves can do?'

'Make you see reason.'

'I doubt it.'

'Well, it's worth a try.'

Further chit-chat was suspended till Jeeves arrived and silence fell except for the ancestor snorting from time to time and self breathing more heavily than usual, for I was much stirred. It always stirs a nephew to discover that a loved aunt does not know the difference between right and wrong. There *is* a difference . . . at my private school Arnold Abney MA used to rub it into the student body both Sundays and weekdays . . . but apparently nobody had told the aged relative about it, with the result that she could purloin people's porringers without a yip from her conscience. Shook me a bit, I confess.

When Jeeves blew in, it cheered me to see the way his head stuck out at the back, for that's where the brain is, and what was needed here was a man with plenty of the old grey matter who would put his points so that even a fermenting aunt would have to be guided by him.

'Well, here's Jeeves,' said the ancestor. 'Tell him the facts and I'll bet he says I've done the only possible thing and can carry on along the lines I sketched out.'

I might have risked a fiver on this at say twelve to eight, but it didn't seem fitting. But telling Jeeves the facts was a good idea, and I did so without delay, being careful to lay a proper foundation.

'Jeeves,' I said.

'Sir?' he responded.

'Sorry to interrupt you again. Were you reading Spinoza?'

'No, sir, I was writing a letter to my Uncle Charlie.'

'Charlie Silversmith,' I explained in an aside to the ancestor. 'Butler at Deverill Hall. One of the best.'

'Thank you, sir.'

'I know few men whom I esteem more highly than your Uncle Charlie. Well, we won't keep you long. It's just that another problem presenting certain points of interest has come up. In a recent conversation I revealed to you the situation relating to Tuppy Glossop and L. P. Runkle. You recall?'

'Yes, sir. Madam was hoping to extract a certain sum of money from Mr Runkle on Mr Glossop's behalf.'

'Exactly. Well, it didn't come off.'

'I am sorry to hear that, sir.'

'But not, I imagine, surprised. If I remember, you considered it a hundred to one shot.'

'Approximately that, sir.'

'Runkle being short of bowels of compassion.'

'Precisely, sir. A twenty-minute egg.'

Here the ancestor repeated her doubts with regard to L. P. Runkle's legitimacy, and would, I think, have developed the theme had I not shushed her down with a raised hand.

'She pleaded in vain,' I said. 'He sent her away with a flea in her ear. I wouldn't be surprised to learn that he laughed her to scorn.'

'The superfatted old son of a bachelor,' the ancestor interposed, and once more I shushed her down.

'Well, you know what happens when you do that sort of thing to a woman of spirit. Thoughts of reprisals fill her mind. And so, coming to the nub, she decided to purloin Runkle's porringer. But I mustn't mislead you. She did this not as an act of vengeance, if you know what I mean, but in order to have a bargaining point when she renewed her application. "Brass up," she would have said when once more urging him to scare the moths out of his pocketbook, "or you won't get back your porringer". Do I make myself clear?'

'Perfectly clear, sir. I find you very lucid.'

'Now first it will have to be explained to you what a porringer is, and here I am handicapped by not having the foggiest notion myself, except that it's silver and old and the sort of thing Uncle Tom has in his collection. Runkle was hoping to sell it to him. Could you supply any details?' I asked the aged relative.

She knitted the brows a bit, and said she couldn't do much in that direction.

'All I know is that it was made in the time of Charles the Second by some Dutchman or other.'

'Then I think I know the porringer to which you allude, sir,' said Jeeves, his face lighting up as much as it ever lights up, he for reasons of his own preferring at all times to preserve the impassivity of a waxwork at Madame Tussaud's. 'It was featured in a Sotheby's catalogue at which I happened to be glancing not long ago. Would it,' he asked the ancestor, 'be a silver-gilt porringer on a circular moulded foot, the lower part chased with acanthus foliage, with beaded scroll handles, the cover surmounted by a foliage on a rosette of swirling acanthus leaves, the stand of tazza form on circular detachable feet with acanthus border joined to a multifoil plate, the palin top with upcurved rim?'

He paused for a reply, but the ancestor did not speak immediately, her aspect that of one who has been run over by a municipal tram. Odd, really, because she must have been listening to that sort of thing from Uncle Tom for years. Finally she mumbled that she wouldn't be surprised or she wouldn't wonder or something like that.

'Your guess is as good as mine,' she said.

'I fancy it must be the same, madam. You mentioned a workman of Dutch origin. Would the name be Hans Conrael Brechtel of the Hague?'

'I couldn't tell you. I know it wasn't Smith or Jones or Robinson, and that's as far as I go. But what's all this in aid of ? What does it matter if the stand is of tazza form or if the palin top has an upcurved rim?'

'Exactly,' I said, thoroughly concurring. 'Or if the credit for these tazza forms and palin tops has to be chalked up to Hans Conrael Brechtel of the Hague. The point, Jeeves, is not what particular porringer the ancestor has pinched, but how far she was justified in pinching any porringer at all when its owner was a guest of hers. I hold that it was a breach of hospitality and the thing must be returned. Am I right?'

'Well, sir . . .'

'Go on, Jeeves,' said the ancestor. 'Say I'm a crook who ought to be drummed out of the Market Snodsbury Ladies Social and Cultural Garden Club.'

'Not at all, madam.'

'Then what were you going to say when you hesitated?'

'Merely that in my opinion no useful end will be served by retaining the object.'

'I don't follow you. How about that bargaining point?'

'It will, I fear, avail you little, madam. As I understand Mr Wooster, the sum you are hoping to obtain from Mr Runkle amounts to a good many thousand pounds.'

'Fifty at least, if not a hundred.'

'Then I cannot envisage him complying with your demands. Mr Runkle is a shrewd financier –'

'Born out of wedlock.'

'Very possibly you are right, madam, nevertheless he is a man well versed in weighing profit and loss. According to Sotheby's catalogue the price at which the object was sold at the auction sale was nine thousand pounds. He will scarcely disburse a hundred or even fifty thousand in order to recover it.'

'Of course he won't,' I said, as enchanted with his lucidity as he had been with mine. It was the sort of thing you have to pay topnotchers at the Bar a king's ransom for. 'He'll simply say "Easy come, easy go" and write it off as a business loss, possibly consulting his legal adviser as to whether he can deduct it from his income tax. Thank you, Jeeves. You've straightened everything out in your customary masterly manner. You're a . . . what were you saying the other day about Daniel somebody?'

'A Daniel come to judgment, sir?'

'That was it. You're a Daniel come to judgment.'

'It is very kind of you to say so, sir.'

'Not at all. Well-deserved tribute.'

I shot a glance at the aged relative. It is notoriously difficult to change the trend of an aunt's mind when that mind is made up about this or that, but I could see at a g. that Jeeves had done it. I hadn't expected her to look pleased, and she didn't, but it was evident that she had accepted what is sometimes called the inevitable. I would describe her as not having a word to say, had she not at this moment said one, suitable enough for the hunting field but on the strong side for mixed company. I registered it in my memory as something to say to Spode some time, always provided it was on the telephone.

'I suppose you're right, Jeeves,' she said, heavy-hearted, though bearing up stoutly. 'It seemed a good idea at the time, but I agree with you that it isn't as watertight as I thought it. It's so often that way with one's golden dreams. The –'

'– best-laid plans of mice and men gang aft agley,' I said helping her out. 'See the poet Burns. I've often wondered why Scotsmen say "gang". I asked you once, Jeeves, if you recall, and you said they had not confided in you. You were saying, ancestor?'

'I was about to say –'

'Or, for that matter, "agley".'

'I was about to say –'

'Or "aft" for "often".'

'I was about to say,' said the relative, having thrown her Rex Stout at me, fortunately with a less accurate aim than the other time, 'that there's nothing to be done but for me to put the thing back in Runkle's room where I took it from.'

'Whence I took it' would have been better, but it was not to comment on her prose style that I interposed. I was thinking that if she was allowed to do the putting back, she might quite possibly change her mind on the way to Runkle's room and decide to stick to the loot after all. Jeeves's arguments had been convincing to the last drop, but you can never be sure that the effect of convincing arguments won't wear off, especially with aunts who don't know the difference between right and wrong, and it might be that she would take the view that if she pocketed the porringer and kept it among her souvenirs, she would at least be saving something from the wreck. 'Always difficult to know what to give Tom for his birthday,' she might say to herself. 'This will be just the thing.'

'I'll do it,' I said. 'Unless you'd rather, Jeeves.'

'No, thank you, sir.'

'Only take a minute of your time.'

'No, thank you, sir.'

'Then you may leave us, Jeeves. Much obliged for your Daniel come to judgmenting.'

'A pleasure, sir.'

'Give Uncle Charlie my love.'

'I will indeed, sir.'

As the door closed behind him, I started to make my plans and dispositions, as I believe the word is, and I found the blood relation docile and helpful. Runkle's room, she told me, was the one known as the Blue Room, and the porringer should be inserted in the left top drawer of the chest of drawers, whence she had removed it. I asked if she was sure he was still in the hammock, and she said he must be, because on her departure he was bound to have gone to sleep again. Taking a line through the cat Augustus, I found this plausible. With these traumatic symplegia cases waking is never more than a temporary thing. I have known Augustus to resume his slumbers within fifteen seconds of having had a shopping bag containing tins of cat food fall on him. A stifled oath, and he was off to dreamland once more.

As I climbed the stairs, I was impressed by the fact that L. P. Runkle had been given the Blue Room, for in this house it amounted to getting star billing. It was the

biggest and most luxurious of the rooms allotted to
bachelors. I once suggested to the aged relative that I be
put there, but all she said was '*You?*' and the
conversation turned to other topics. Runkle having got it
in spite of the presence on the premises of a seventh Earl
showed how determined the a. r. had been that no stone
should be left unturned and no avenue unexplored in her
efforts to soften him up; and it seemed ironical that all
her carefully thought-out plans should have gone agley.
Just shows Burns knew what he was talking about. You
can generally rely on these poets to hit the mark and
entitle themselves to a cigar or coconut according to
choice.

The old sweats will remember, though later arrivals
will have to be told, that this was not the first time I had
gone on a secret mission to the Blue Room. That other
visit, the old sweats will recall, had ended in disaster
and not knowing which way to look, for Mrs Homer
Cream, the well-known writer of suspense novels, had
found me on the floor with a chair round my neck, and
it had not been easy to explain. This was no doubt why
on the present occasion I approached the door with
emotions somewhat similar to those I had had in the old
days when approaching that of Arnold Abney MA at the
conclusion of morning prayers. A voice seemed to
whisper in my ear that beyond that door there lurked
something that wasn't going to do me a bit of good.

The voice was perfectly right. It had got its facts
correct first shot. What met my eyes as I entered was
L. P. Runkle asleep on the bed, and with my customary
quickness I divined what must have happened. After
being cornered there by the old ancestor he must have
come to the conclusion that a hammock out in the
middle of a lawn, with access to it from all directions,
was no place for a man who wanted peace and seclusion,
and that these were to be obtained only in his bedroom.
Thither, accordingly, he had gone, and there he was.

Voilà tout, as one might say if one had made a study of the French language.

The sight of this sleeping beauty had, of course, given me a nasty start, causing my heart to collide rather violently with my front teeth, but it was only for a moment that I was unequal to what I have heard Jeeves call the intellectual pressure of the situation. It is pretty generally recognized in the circles in which I move that Bertram Wooster, though he may be down, is never out, the betting being odds on that, given time to collect his thoughts and stop his head spinning, he will rise on stepping stones of his dead self to higher things, as the fellow said, and it was so now. I would have preferred, of course, to operate in a room wholly free from the presence of L. P. Runkle, but I realized that as long as he remained asleep there was nothing to keep me from carrying on. All that was required was that my activities should be conducted in absolute silence. And it was thus that I was conducting them, more like a spectre or wraith than a chartered member of the Drones Club, when the air was rent, as the expression is, by a sharp yowl such as you hear when a cougar or a snow leopard stubs its toe on a rock, and I became aware that I had trodden on the cat Augustus, who had continued to follow me, still, I suppose, under the mistaken impression that I had kippered herrings on my person and might at any moment start loosening up.

In normal circumstances I would have hastened to make my apologies and to endeavour by tickling him behind the ear to apply balm to his wounded feelings, but at this moment L. P. Runkle sat up, said 'Wah-wah-wah', rubbed his eyes, gave me an unpleasant look with them and asked me what the devil I was doing in his room.

It was not an easy question to answer. There had been nothing in our relations since we first swam into each other's ken to make it seem likely that I had come to smooth his pillow or ask him if he would like a cooling drink, and I did not put forward these explanations. I was thinking how right the ancestor had been in predicting that, if aroused suddenly, he would wake up cross. His whole demeanour was that of a man who didn't much like the human race as a whole but was particularly allergic to Woosters. Not even Spode could have made his distaste for them plainer.

I decided to see what could be done with suavity. It had answered well in the case of Ginger, and there was no saying that it might not help to ease the current situation.

'I'm sorry,' I said with an enchanting smile, 'I'm afraid I woke you.'

'Yes, you did. And stop grinning at me like a half-witted ape.'

'Right-ho,' I said. I removed the enchanting smile. It came off quite easily. 'I don't wonder you're annoyed. But I'm more to be pitied than censured. I inadvertently trod on the cat.'

A look of alarm spread over his face. It had a long way to go, but it spread all right.

'Hat?' he quavered, and I could see that he feared for the well-being of his Panama with the pink ribbon.

I lost no time in reassuring him.

'Not hat. Cat.'

'What cat?'

'Oh, haven't you met? Augustus his name is, though for purposes of conversation this is usually shortened to Gus. He and I have been buddies since he was a kitten. He must have been following me when I came in here.'

It was an unfortunate way of putting it, for it brought him back to his original theme.

'Why the devil did you come in here?'

A lesser man than Bertram Wooster would have been non-plussed, and I don't mind admitting that I was, too, for about a couple of ticks. But as I stood shuffling the

feet and twiddling the fingers I caught sight of that
camera of his standing on an adjacent table, and I got
one of those inspirations you get occasionally.
Shakespeare and Burns and even Oliver Wendell Holmes
probably used to have them all the time, but self not so
often. In fact, this was the first that had come my way
for some weeks.

'Aunt Dahlia sent me to ask you if you would come
and take a few photographs of her and the house and all
that sort of thing, so that she'll have them to look at in
the long winter evenings. You know how long the
winter evenings get nowadays.'

The moment I had said it I found myself speculating
as to whether the inspiration had been as hot as I had
supposed. I mean, this man had just had a conference
with the old ancestor which, unlike those between
ministers of state, had not been conducted in an
atmosphere of the utmost cordiality, and he might be
thinking it odd that so soon after its conclusion she
should be wanting him to take photographs of her. But
all was well. No doubt he looked on her request as what
is known as an olive branch. Anyway, he was all
animation and eagerness to co-operate.

'I'll be right down,' he said. 'Tell her I'll be right
down.'

Having hidden the porringer in my room and locked
the door, I went back to the aged relative and found her
with Jeeves. She expressed relief at seeing me.

'Oh, there you are, my beautiful bounding Bertie.
Thank goodness you didn't go to Runkle's room. Jeeves
tells me Seppings met Runkle on the stairs and he asked
him to bring him a cup of tea in half an hour. He said he
was going to lie down. You might have run right into
him.'

I laughed one of those hollow, mirthless ones.

'Jeeves speaks too late, old ancestor. I did run into
him.'

'You mean he was *there*?'

'With his hair in a braid.'

'What did you do?'

'I told him you had asked me to ask him to come and take some photographs.'

'Quick thinking.'

'I always think like lightning.'

'And did he swallow it?'

'He appeared to. He said he would be right down.'

'Well, I'm damned if I'm going to smile.'

Whether I would have pleaded with her to modify this stern resolve and at least show a portion of her front teeth when Runkle pressed the button, I cannot say, for as she spoke my thoughts were diverted. A sudden query presented itself. What, I asked myself, was keeping L. P. Runkle? He had said he would be right down, but quite a time had elapsed and no sign of him. I was toying with the idea that on a warm afternoon like this a man of his build might have had a fit of some kind, when there came from the stairs the sound of clumping feet, and he was with us.

But a very different L. P. Runkle from the man who had told me he would be right down. Then he had been all sunny and beaming, the amateur photographer who was not only going to make a pest of himself by taking photographs but had actually been asked to make a pest of himself in this manner, which seldom happens to amateur photographers. Now he was cold and hard like a picnic egg, and he couldn't have looked at me with more loathing if I really had trodden on his Panama hat.

'Mrs Travers!'

His voice had rung out with the clarion note of a costermonger seeking to draw the attention of the purchasing public to his blood oranges and Brussels sprouts. I saw the ancestor stiffen, and I knew she was about to go into her *grande dame* act. This relative, though in ordinary circs so genial and matey, can on occasion turn in a flash into a carbon copy of a Duchess of the old school reducing an underling to a spot of grease, and what is so remarkable is that she doesn't have to use a lorgnette, just does it all with the power of the human eye. I think girls in her day used to learn the trick at their finishing schools.

'Will you kindly not bellow at me, Mr Runkle. I am not deaf. What is it?'

The aristocratic ice in her tone sent a cold shiver down my spine, but in L. P. Runkle she had picked a tough customer to try to freeze. He apologized for having bellowed, but briefly and with no real contrition. He then proceeded to deal with her query as to what it was, and with a powerful effort forced himself to speak quite quietly. Not exactly like a cooing pigeon, but quietly.

'I wonder if you remember, Mrs Travers, a silver porringer I showed you on my arrival here.'

'I do.'

'Very valuable.'

'So you told me.'

'I kept it in the top left-hand drawer of the chest of drawers in my bedroom. It did not occur to me that there was any necessity to hide it. I took the honesty of everybody under your roof for granted.'

'Naturally.'

'Even when I found that Mr Wooster was one of my fellow guests I took no precautions. It was a fatal blunder. He has just stolen it.'

I suppose it's pretty much of a strain to keep up that *grande dame* stuff for any length of time, involving as it does rigidity of the facial muscles and the spinal column, for at these words the ancestor called it a day and reverted to the Quorn-and-Pytchleyness of her youth.

'Don't be a damned fool, Runkle. You're talking rot. Bertie would never dream of doing such a thing, would you, Bertie?'

'Not in a million years.'

'The man's an ass.'

'One might almost say a silly ass.'

'Comes of sleeping all the time.'

'I believe that's the trouble.'

'Addles the brain.'

'Must, I imagine. It's the same thing with Gus the cat. I love Gus like a brother, but after years of non-stop sleep he's got about as much genuine intelligence as a Cabinet minister.'

'I hope Runkle hasn't annoyed you with his preposterous allegations?'

'No, no, old ancestor, I'm not angry, just terribly terribly hurt.'

You'd have thought all this would have rendered Runkle a spent force and a mere shell of his former self, but his eye was not dimmed nor his natural force abated. Turning to the door, he paused there to add a few words.

'I disagree with you, Mrs Travers, in the view you take of your nephew's honesty. I prefer to be guided by Lord Sidcup, who assures me that Mr Wooster invariably steals anything that is not firmly fastened to the floor. It was only by the merest chance, Lord Sidcup tells me, that at their first meeting he did not make away with an umbrella belonging to Sir Watkyn Bassett, and from there he has, as one might put it, gone from strength to strength. Umbrellas, cow-creamers, amber statuettes, cameras, all are grist to his mill. I was unfortunately asleep when he crept into my room, and he had plenty of time before I woke to do what he had come for. It was only some minutes after he had slunk out that it occurred to me to look in the top left-hand drawer of my chest of drawers. My suspicions were confirmed. The drawer was empty. He had got away with the swag. But I am a man of action. I have sent your butler to the police station to bring a constable to search Wooster's room. I, until he arrives, propose to stand outside it, making sure that he does not go in and tamper with the evidence.'

Having said which in the most unpleasant of vocal deliveries, L. P. Runkle became conspic. by his a., and the ancestor spoke with considerable eloquence on the subject of fat slobs of dubious parentage who had the immortal crust to send her butler on errands. I, too, was exercised by the concluding portion of his remarks.

'I don't like that,' I said, addressing Jeeves, who during the recent proceedings had been standing in the background giving a lifelike impersonation of somebody who wasn't there.

'Sir?'

'If the fuzz search my room, I'm sunk.'

'Have no anxiety, sir. A police officer is not permitted to enter private property without authority, nor do the regulations allow him to ask the owner of such property for permission to enter.'

'You're sure of that?'

'Yes, sir.'

Well, that was a crumb of comfort, but it would be deceiving my public if I said that Bertram Wooster was his usual nonchalant self. Too many things had been happening one on top of the other for him to be the carefree boulevardier one likes to see. If I hoped to clarify the various situations which were giving me the pip and erase the dark circles already beginning to form beneath the eyes, it would, I saw, be necessary for me to marshal my thoughts.

'Jeeves,' I said, leading him from the room, 'I must marshal my thoughts.'

'Certainly, sir, if you wish.'

'And I can't possibly do it here with crises turning handsprings on every side. Can you think of a good excuse for me to pop up to London for the night? A few hours alone in the peaceful surroundings of the flat are what I need. I must concentrate, concentrate.'

'But do you require an excuse, sir?'

'It's better to have one. Aunt Dahlia is on a sticky wicket and would be hurt if I deserted her now unless I had some good reason. I can't let her down.'

'The sentiment does you credit, sir.'

'Thank you, Jeeves. Can you think of anything?'

'You have been summoned for jury duty, sir.'

'Don't they let you have a longish notice for that?'

'Yes, sir, but when the post arrived containing the letter from the authorities, I forgot to give it to you, and only delivered it a moment ago. Fortunately it was not too late. Would you be intending to leave immediately?'

'If not sooner. I'll borrow Ginger's car.'

'You will miss the debate, sir.'

'The what?'

'The debate between Mr Winship and his opponent. It takes place tomorrow night.'

'What time?'

'It is scheduled for a quarter to seven.'

'Taking how long?'

'Perhaps an hour.'

'Then expect me back at about seven-thirty. The great thing in life, Jeeves, if we wish to be happy and prosperous, is to miss as many political debates as possible. You wouldn't care to come with me, would you?'

'No, thank you, sir. I am particularly anxious to hear Mr Winship's speech.'

'He'll probably only say "Er",' I riposted rather cleverly.

16

It was with a heart-definitely-bowed-down mood and the circles beneath my eyes darker than ever that I drove back next day in what is known as the quiet evenfall. I remember Jeeves saying something to me once about the heavy and the weary weight of this unintelligible world ... not his own, I gathered, but from the works of somebody called Wordsworth, if I caught the name correctly ... and it seemed to me rather a good way of describing the depressing feeling you get when the soup is about to close over you and no life-belt is in sight. I was conscious of·this heavy and weary weight some years ago, that time when my cousins Eustace and Claude without notifying me inserted twenty-three cats in my bedroom, and I had it again, in spades, at the present juncture.

Consider the facts. I had gone up to London to wrestle in solitude with the following problems:

(a) How am I to get out of marrying Madeline Bassett?
(b) How am I to restore the porringer to L. P. Runkle before the constabulary come piling on the back of my neck?
(c) How is the ancestor to extract that money from Runkle?
(d) How is Ginger to marry Magnolia Glendennon while betrothed to Florence?

and I was returning with all four still in status quo. For a night and day I had been giving them the cream of the Wooster brain, and for all I had accomplished I might have been the aged relative trying to solve the *Observer* crossword puzzle.

Arriving at journey's end, I steered the car into the drive. About half-way along it there was a tricky right-hand turn, and I had slowed down to negotiate this, when a dim figure appeared before me, a voice said, 'Hoy!', and I saw that it was Ginger.

He seemed annoyed about something. His 'Hoy!' had had a note of reproach in it, as far as it is possible to get the note of reproach into a 'Hoy!', and as he drew near and shoved his torso through the window I received the distinct impression that he was displeased.

His opening words confirmed this.

'Bertie, you abysmal louse, what's kept you all this time? When I lent you my car, I didn't expect you'd come back at two o'clock in the morning.'

'It's only half-past seven.'

He seemed amazed.

'Is that all? I thought it was later. So much has been happening.'

'What has been happening?'

'No time to tell you now. I'm in a hurry.'

It was at this point that I noticed something in his appearance which I had overlooked. A trifle, but I'm rather observant.

'You've got egg in your hair,' I said.

'Of course I've got egg in my hair,' he said, his manner betraying impatience. 'What did you expect me to have in my hair, Chanel Number Five?'

'Did somebody throw an egg at you?'

'Everybody threw eggs at everybody. Correction. Some of them threw turnips and potatoes.'

'You mean the meeting broke up in disorder, as the expression is?'

'I don't suppose any meeting in the history of English politics has ever broken up in more disorder. Eggs flew hither and thither. The air was dark with vegetables of every description. Sidcup got a black eye. Somebody plugged him with a potato.'

I found myself in two minds. On the one hand I felt a pang of regret for having missed what had all the earmarks of having been a political meeting of the most rewarding kind: on the other, it was like rare and refreshing fruit to hear that Spode had got hit in the eye with a potato. I was conscious of an awed respect for the marksman who had accomplished this feat. A potato, being so nobbly in shape, can be aimed accurately only by a master hand.

'Tell me more,' I said, well pleased.

'Tell you more be blowed. I've got to get up to London. We want to be there bright and early tomorrow in order to inspect registrars and choose the best one.'

This didn't sound like Florence, who, if she ever gets through an engagement without breaking it, is sure to insist on a wedding with bishops, bridesmaids, full choral effects, and a reception afterwards. A sudden thought struck me, and I think I may have gasped. Somebody made a noise like a dying soda-water syphon and it was presumably me.

'When you say "we", do you mean you and M. Glendennon?'

'Who else?'

'But how?'

'Never mind how.'

'But I do mind how. You were Problem (d) on my list, and I want to know how you have been solved. I gather that Florence has remitted your sentence –'

'She has, in words of unmistakable clarity. Get out of that car.'

'But why?'

'Because if you aren't out of it in two seconds, I'm going to pull you out.'

'I mean why did she r. your s.?'

'Ask Jeeves,' he said, and attaching himself to the collar of my coat he removed me from the automobile like a stevedore hoisting a sack of grain. He took my place at the wheel, and disappeared down the drive to keep his tryst with the little woman, who presumably awaited him at some prearranged spot with the bags and baggage.

He left me in a condition which can best be described as befogged, bewildered, mystified, confused and perplexed. All I had got out of him was (a) that the debate had not been conducted in an atmosphere of the utmost cordiality, (b) that at its conclusion Florence had forbidden the banns and (c) that if I wanted further information Jeeves would supply it. A little more than the charmers got out of the deaf adder, but not much. I felt like a barrister, as it might be Ma McCorkadale, who has been baffled by an unsatisfactory witness.

However, he had spoken of Jeeves as a fount of information, so my first move on reaching the drawing-room and finding no one there was to put forefinger to bell button and push.

Seppings answered the summons. He and I have been buddies from boyhood – mine, of course, not his – and as a rule when we meet conversation flows like water, mainly on the subject of the weather and the state of his lumbago, but this was no time for idle chatter.

'Seppings,' I said, 'I want Jeeves. Where is he?'

'In the Servants' Hall, sir, comforting the parlourmaid.'

I took him to allude to the employee whose gong-work I had admired on my first evening, and, pressing though my business was, it seemed only humane to offer a word of sympathy for whatever her misfortunes might be.

'Had bad news, has she?'

'No, sir, she was struck by a turnip.'

'Where?'

'In the lower ribs, sir.'

'I mean where did this happen?'

'At the Town Hall, sir, in the later stages of the debate.'

I drew in the breath sharply. More and more I was beginning to realize that the meeting I had missed had been marked by passions which recalled the worst excesses of the French Revolution.

'I myself, sir, narrowly escaped being hit by a tomato. It whizzed past my ear.'

'You shock me profoundly, Seppings. I don't wonder you're pale and trembling.' And indeed he was, like a badly set blancmange. 'What caused all this turmoil?'

'Mr Winship's speech, sir.'

This surprised me. I could readily believe that any speech of Ginger's would be well below the mark set by Demosthenes, if that really was the fellow's name, but surely not so supremely lousy as to start his audience throwing eggs and vegetables; and I was about to institute further enquiries, when Seppings sidled to the door, saying that he would inform Mr Jeeves of my desire to confer with him. And in due season the hour produced the man, as the expression is.

'You wished to see me, sir?' he said.

'You can put it even stronger, Jeeves. I yearned to see you.'

'Indeed, sir?'

'Just now I met Ginger in the drive.'

'Yes, sir, he informed me that he was going there to await your return.'

'He tells me he is no longer betrothed to Miss Craye, being now affianced to Miss Glendennon. And when I asked him how this switch had come about, he said that you would explain.'

'I shall be glad to do so, sir. You wish a complete report?'

'That's right. Omit no detail, however slight.'

He was silent for a space. Marshalling his thoughts, no doubt. Then he got down to it.

'The importance attached by the electorate to the debate,' he began, 'was very evident. An audience of considerable size had assembled in the Town Hall. The Mayor and Corporation were there, together with the flower of Market Snodsbury's aristocracy and a rougher element in cloth caps and turtleneck sweaters who should never have been admitted.'

I had to rebuke him at this point.

'Bit snobbish, that, Jeeves, what? You are a little too inclined to judge people by their clothes. Turtleneck sweaters are royal raiment when they're worn for virtue's sake, and a cloth cap may hide an honest heart. Probably frightfully good chaps, if one had got to know them.'

'I would prefer not to know them, sir. It was they who subsequently threw eggs, potatoes, tomatoes and turnips.'

I had to concede that he had a point there.

'True,' I said. 'I was forgetting that. All right, Jeeves. Carry on.'

'The proceedings opened with a rendering of the national anthem by the boys and girls of Market Snodsbury elementary school.'

'Pretty ghastly, I imagine?'

'Somewhat revolting, sir.'

'And then?'

'The Mayor made a short address, introducing the contestants, and Mrs McCorkadale rose to speak. She was wearing a smart coat in fine quality repp over a long-sleeved frock of figured marocain pleated at the sides and finished at the neck with –'

'Skip all that, Jeeves.'

'I am sorry, sir. I thought you wished every detail, however slight.'

'Only when they're . . . what's the word?'

'Pertinent, sir?'

'That's right. Take the McCorkadale's outer crust as read. How was her speech?'

'Extremely telling, in spite of a good deal of heckling.'

'That wouldn't put her off her stroke.'

'No, sir. She impressed me as being of a singularly forceful character.'

'Me, too.'

'You have met the lady, sir?'

'For a few minutes – which, however, were plenty. She spoke at some length?'

'Yes, sir. If you would care to read her remarks? I took down both speeches in shorthand.'

'Later on, perhaps.'

'At any time that suits you, sir.'

'And how was the applause? Hearty? Or sporadic?'

'On one side of the hall extremely hearty. The rougher element appeared to be composed in almost equal parts of her supporters and those of Mr Winship. They had been seated at opposite sides of the auditorium, no doubt by design. Her supporters cheered, Mr Winship's booed.'

'And when Ginger got up, I suppose her lot booed him?'

'No doubt they would have done so, had it not been for the tone of his address. His appearance was greeted with a certain modicum of hostility, but he had scarcely begun to speak when he was rapturously received.'

'By the opposition?'

'Yes, sir.'

'Strange.'

'Yes, sir.'

'Can you elucidate?'

'Yes, sir. If I might consult my notes for a moment. Ah, yes. Mr Winship's opening words were, "Ladies and gentlemen, I come before you a changed man." A Voice:

"That's good news." A second Voice: "Shut up, you
bleeder." A third Voice . . .'

'I think we might pass lightly over the Voices, Jeeves.'

'Very good, sir. Mr Winship then said, "I should like
to begin with a word to the gentleman in the turtleneck
sweater in that seat over there who kept calling my
opponent a silly old geezer. If he will kindly step on to
this platform. I shall be happy to knock his ugly block
off. Mrs McCorkadale is *not* a silly old geezer." A Voice
. . . Excuse me, sir, I was forgetting. "Mrs McCorkadale
is *not* a silly old geezer," Mr Winship said, "but a lady of
the greatest intelligence and grasp of affairs. I admire her
intensely. Listening to her this evening has changed my
political views completely. She has converted me to
hers, and I propose, when the polls are opened, to cast
my vote for her. I advise all of you to do the same.
Thank you." He then resumed his seat.'

'Good Lord, Jeeves!'

'Yes, sir.'

'He really said that?'

'Yes, sir.'

'No wonder his engagement's off.'

'I must confess it occasioned me no surprise, sir.'

I continued amazed. It seemed incredible that Ginger,
whose long suit was muscle rather than brain, should
have had the ingenuity and know-how to think up such
a scheme for freeing himself from Florence's clutches
without forfeiting his standing as a fairly *preux
chevalier*. It seemed to reveal him as possessed of
snakiness of a high order, and I was just thinking that
you never can tell about a fellow's hidden depths, when
one of those sudden thoughts of mine came popping to
the surface.

'Was this you, Jeeves?'

'Sir?'

'Did you put Ginger up to doing it?'

'It is conceivable that Mr Winship may have been

influenced by something I said, sir. He was very much exercised with regard to his matrimonial entanglements and he did me the honour of consulting me. It is quite possible that I may have let fall some careless remark that turned his thoughts in the direction they took.'

'In other words, you told him to go to it?'

'Yes, sir.'

I was silent for a space. I was thinking how jolly it would be if he could dish up something equally effective with regard to me and M. Bassett. The thought also occurred to me that what had happened, while excellent for Ginger, wasn't so good for his backers and supporters and the Conservative cause in general.

I mentioned this.

'Tough on the fellows who betted on him.'

'Into each life some rain must fall, sir.'

'Though possibly a good thing. A warning to them in future to keep their money in the old oak chest and not risk it on wagers. May prove a turning point in their lives. What really saddens one is the thought that Bingley will now clean up. He'll make a packet.'

'He told me this afternoon that he was expecting to do so.'

'You mean you've seen him?'

'He came here at about five o'clock, sir.'

'Stockish, hard and full of rage, I suppose?'

'On the contrary, sir, extremely friendly. He made no allusion to the past. I gave him a cup of tea, and we chatted for perhaps half an hour.'

'Strange.'

'Yes, sir. I wondered if he might not have had an ulterior motive in approaching me.'

'Such as?'

'I must confess I cannot think of one. Unless he entertained some hope of inducing me to part with the club book, but that is hardly likely. Would there be anything further, sir?'

'You want to get back to the stricken parlourmaid?'

'Yes, sir. When you rang, I was about to see what a little weak brandy and water would do.'

I sped him on his errand of mercy and sat down to brood. You might have supposed that the singular behaviour of Bingley would have occupied my thoughts. I mean, when you hear that a chap of his well-established crookedness has been acting oddly, your natural impulse is to say 'Aha!' and wonder what his game is. And perhaps for a minute or two I did ponder on this. But I had so many other things to ponder on that Bingley soon got shoved into the discard. If I remember rightly, it was as I mused on Problem (b), the one about restoring the porringer to L. P. Runkle, and again drew a blank, that my reverie was interrupted by the entrance of the old ancestor.

She was wearing the unmistakable look of an aunt who has just been having the time of her life, and this did not surprise me. Hers since she sold the weekly paper she used to run, the one I did that piece on What The Well-Dressed Man Will Wear for, has been a quiet sort of existence, pleasant enough but lacking in incident and excitement. A really sensational event such as the egg-and-vegetable-throwing get-together she had just been present at must have bucked her up like a week at the seaside.

Her greeting could not have been more cordial. An aunt's love oozed out from every syllable.

'Hullo, you revolting object,' she said. 'So you're back.'

'Just arrived.'

'Too bad you had that jury job. You missed a gripping experience.'

'So Jeeves was telling me.'

'Ginger finally went off his rocker.'

With the inside information which had been placed at my disposal I was able to correct this view.

'It was no rocker that he went off, aged relative. His actions were motivated by the soundest good sense. He wanted to get Florence out of his hair without actually telling her to look elsewhere for a mate.'

'Don't be an ass. He loves her.'

'No longer. He's switched to Magnolia Glendennon.'

'You mean that secretary of his?'

'That identical secretary.'

'How do you know?'

'He told me so himself.'

'Well, I'll be blowed. He finally got fed up with Florence's bossiness, did he?'

'Yes, I think it must have been coming on for some time without him knowing it, subconsciously as Jeeves would say. Meeting Magnolia brought it to the surface.'

'She seems a nice girl.'

'Very nice, according to Ginger.'

'I must congratulate him.'

'You'll have to wait a bit. They've gone up to London.'

'So have Spode and Madeline. And Runkle ought to be leaving soon. It's like one of those great race movements of the Middle Ages I used to read about at school. Well, this is wonderful. Pretty soon it'll be safe for Tom to return to the nest. There's still Florence, of course, but I doubt if she will be staying on. My cup runneth over, young Bertie. I've missed Tom sorely. Home's not home without him messing about the place. Why are you staring at me like a halibut on a fishmonger's slab?'

I had not been aware that I was conveying this resemblance to the fish she mentioned, but my gaze had certainly been on the intent side, for her opening words had stirred me to my depths.

'Did you say,' I – yes, I suppose, vociferated would be the word, 'that Spode and Madeline Bassett had gone to London?'

'Left half an hour ago.'

'Together?'

'Yes, in his car.'

'But Spode told me she had given him the push.'

'She did, but everything's all right again. He's not going to give up his title and stand for Parliament. Getting hit in the eye with that potato changed his plans completely. It made him feel that if that was the sort of thing you have to go through to get elected to the House of Commons, he preferred to play it safe and stick to the House of Lords. And she, of course, assured that there was going to be no funny business and that she would become the Countess of Sidcup all right, withdrew her objections to marrying him. Now you're puffing like Tom when he goes upstairs too fast. Why is this?'

Actually, I had breathed deeply, not puffed, and certainly not like Uncle Tom when he goes upstairs too fast, but I suppose to an aunt there isn't much difference between a deep-breathing nephew and a puffing nephew, and anyway I was in no mood to discuss the point.

'You don't know who it was who threw that potato, do you?' I asked.

'The one that hit Spode? I don't. It sort of came out of the void. Why?'

'Because if I knew who it was, I would send camels bearing apes, ivory and peacocks to his address. He saved me from the fate that is worse than death. I allude to marriage with the Bassett disaster.'

'Was she going to marry you?'

'According to Spode.'

A look almost of awe came into the ancestor's face.

'How right you were,' she said, 'when you told me once that you had faith in your star. I've lost count of the number of times you've been definitely headed for the altar with apparently no hope of evading the firing squad, and every time something has happened which enabled you to wriggle out of it. It's uncanny.'

She would, I think, have gone deeper into the matter, for already she had begun to pay a marked tribute to my guardian angel, who, she said, plainly knew his job from soup to nuts, but at this moment Seppings appeared and asked her if she would have a word with Jeeves, and she went out to have it.

And I had just put my feet up on the chaise longue and was starting to muse ecstatically on the astounding bit of luck which had removed the Bassett menace from my life, when my mood of what the French call *bien être* was given the sleeve across the windpipe by the entrance of L. P. Runkle, the mere sight of whom, circs being what they were, was enough to freeze the blood and make each particular hair stand on end like quills upon the fretful porpentine, as I have heard Jeeves put it.

I wasn't glad to see him, but he seemed glad to see me.

'Oh, there you are,' he said. 'They told me you had skipped. Very sensible of you to come back. It's never any good going on the run, because the police are sure to get you sooner or later, and it makes it all the worse for you if you've done a bolt.'

With cold dignity I said I had had to go up to London on business. He paid no attention to this. He was scrutinizing me rather in the manner of the halibut on the fishmonger's slab to which the ancestor had referred in our recent conversation.

'The odd thing is,' he said, continuing to scan me closely, 'that you haven't a criminal face. It's a silly, fatuous face, but not criminal. You remind me of one of those fellows who do dances with the soubrette in musical comedy.'

Come, come, I said to myself, this is better. Spode had compared me to a member of the ensemble. In the view of L. P. Runkle I was at any rate one of the principals. Moving up in the world.

'Must be a great help to you in your business. Lulls people into a false security. They think there can't be any danger from someone who looks like you, they're off their guard, and *wham*! you've got away with their umbrellas and cameras. No doubt you owe all your successes to this. But you know the old saying about the pitcher going too often to the well. This time you're for it. This time – '

He broke off, not because he had come to an end of his very offensive remarks but because Florence had joined us, and her appearance immediately claimed his attention. She was far from being dapper. It was plain that she had been in the forefront of the late battle, for whereas Ginger had merely had egg in his hair, she was, as it were, festooned in egg. She had evidently been right in the centre of the barrage. In all political meetings of the stormier kind these things are largely a matter of luck. A escapes unscathed, B becomes a human omelette.

A more tactful man than L. P. Runkle would have affected not to notice this, but I don't suppose it ever occurred to him to affect not to notice things.

'Hullo!' he said. 'You've got egg all over you.'

Florence replied rather acidly that she was aware of this.

'Better change your dress.'

'I intend to. Would you mind, Mr Runkle, if I had a word with Mr Wooster alone?'

I think Runkle was on the point of saying 'What about?', but on catching her eye he had prudent second thoughts. He lumbered off, and she proceeded to have the word she had mentioned.

She kept it crisp. None of the 'Er' stuff which was such a feature of Ginger's oratory. Even Demosthenes would have been slower in coming to the nub, though he, of course, would been handicapped by having to speak in Greek.

'I'm glad I found you, Bertie.'

A civil 'Oh, ah' was all the reply I could think of.

'I have been thinking things over, and I have made up my mind. Harold Winship is a mere lout, and I am

having nothing more to do with him. I see now that I
made a great mistake when I broke off my engagement
to you. You have your faults, but they are easily
corrected. I have decided to marry you, and I think we
shall be very happy.'

'But not immediately,' said L. P. Runkle, rejoining us.
I described him a moment ago as lumbering off, but a
man like that never lumbers far if there is a chance of
hearing what somebody has to say to somebody else in
private. 'He'll first have to do a longish stretch in
prison.'

His reappearance had caused Florence to stiffen. She
now stiffened further, her aspect similar to that of the
old ancestor when about to go into her *grande dame* act.

'Mr Runkle!'

'I'm here.'

'I thought you had gone.'

'I hadn't.'

'How dare you listen to a private conversation!'

'They're the only things worth listening to. I owe
much of my large fortune to listening to private
conversations.'

'What is this nonsense about prison?'

'Wooster won't find it nonsense. He has sneaked a
valuable silver porringer of mine, a thing I paid nine
thousand pounds for, and I am expecting a man any
minute now who will produce the evidence necessary to
convict. It's an open and shut case.'

'Is this true, Bertie?' said Florence with that touch of
the prosecuting District Attorney I remembered so
vividly, and all I could say was 'Well . . . I . . . er . . . well.'

With a guardian angel like mine working overtime, it
was enough. She delivered judgment instantaneously.

'I shall not marry you,' she said, and went off
haughtily to de-egg herself.

'Very sensible of her,' said L. P. Runkle. 'The right
course to take. A man like you, bound to be in and out

of prison, couldn't possibly be a good husband. How is a
wife to make her plans . . . dinner parties, holidays,
Christmas treats for the children, the hundred and one
things a woman has to think of . . . when she doesn't
know from one day to another whether the head of the
house won't be telephoning to say he's been arrested
again and no bail allowed? Yes?' said Runkle, and I saw
that Seppings had appeared in the offing.

'A Mr Bingley has called to see you, sir.'

'Ah, yes, I was expecting him.'

He popped off, and scarcely had he ceased to pollute
the atmosphere when the old ancestor blew in.

She was plainly agitated, the resemblance to a cat on
hot bricks being very marked. She panted a good deal,
and her face had taken on the rather pretty mauve colour
it always does when the soul is not at rest.

'Bertie,' she boomed, 'when you went away yesterday,
did you leave the door of your bedroom unlocked?'

'Of course I didn't.'

'Well, Jeeves says it's open now.'

'It can't be.'

'It is. He thinks Runkle or some minion of his has
skeleton-keyed the lock. Don't yell like that, curse you.'

I might have retorted by asking her what she expected
me to do when I suddenly saw all, but I was too busy
seeing all to be diverted into arguments about my voice
production. The awful truth had hit me as squarely
between the eyes as if it had been an egg or a turnip
hurled by one of the Market Snodsbury electorate.

'Bingley!' I ejaculated.

'And don't sing.'

'I was not singing, I was ejaculating "Bingley!", or
vociferating "Bingley!" if you prefer it. You remember
Bingley, the fellow who stole the club book, the chap
you were going to take by the throat and shake like a rat.
Aged relative, we are up against it in no uncertain
manner. Bingley is the Runkle minion you alluded to.

Jeeves says he dropped in to tea this afternoon. What simpler for him, having had his cuppa, than to nip upstairs and search my room? He used to be Runkle's personal attendant, so Runkle would turn to him naturally when he needed an accomplice. Yes, I don't wonder you're perturbed,' I added, for she had set the welkin ringing with one of those pungent monosyllables so often on her lips in the old Quorn-and-Pytchley days. 'And I'll tell you something else which will remove your last doubts, if you had any. He's just turned up again, and Runkle has gone out to confer with him. What do you suppose they're conferring about? Give you three guesses.'

The Quorn trains its daughters well. So does the Pytchley. She did not swoon, as many an aunt would have done in her place, merely repeated the monosyllable in a slightly lower tone – meditatively as it were, like some aristocrat of the French Revolution on being informed that the tumbril waited.

'This tears it,' she said, the very words such an aristocrat would have used, though speaking of course in French. 'I'll have to confess that I took his foul porringer.'

'No, no, you mustn't do that.'

'What else is there for me to do? I can't let you go to chokey.'

'I don't mind.'

'I do. I may have my faults –'

'No, no.'

'Yes, yes. I am quite aware that there are blemishes in my spiritual make-up which ought to have been corrected at my finishing school, but I draw the line at letting my nephew do a stretch for pinching porringers which I pinched myself. That's final.'

I saw what she meant, of course. *Noblesse oblige*, and all that. And very creditable, too. But I had a powerful argument to put forward, and I lost no time in putting it.

'But wait, old ancestor. There's another aspect of the matter. If it's . . . what's the expression? . . . if it's bruited abroad that I'm merely an as-pure-as-the-driven-snow innocent bystander, my engagement to Florence will be on again.'

'Your what to who?' It should have been 'whom', but I let it go. 'Are you telling me that you and Florence . . .'

'She proposed to me ten minutes ago and I had to accept her because one's either *preux* or one isn't, and then Runkle butted in and pointed out to her the disadvantages of marrying someone who would shortly be sewing mailbags in Wormwood Scrubs, and she broke it off.'

The relative seemed stunned, as if she had come on something abstruse in the *Observer* crossword puzzle.

'What is it about you that fascinates the girls? First Madeline Bassett, now Florence, and dozens of others in the past. You must have a magnetic personality.'

'That would seem to be the explanation,' I agreed. 'Anyway, there it is. One whisper that there isn't a stain on my character, and I haven't a hope. The Bishop will be notified, the assistant clergy and bridesmaids rounded up, the organist will start practising "The Voice That Breathed O'er Eden", and the limp figure you see drooping at the altar rails will be Bertram Wilberforce Wooster. I implore you, old blood relation, to be silent and let the law take its course. If it's a choice between serving a life sentence under Florence and sewing a mailbag or two, give me the mailbags every time.'

She nodded understandingly, and said she saw what I meant.

'I thought you would.'

'There is much in what you say.' She mused awhile. 'As a matter of fact, though, I doubt if it will get as far as mailbags. I'm pretty sure what's going to happen. Runkle will offer to drop the whole thing if I let him have Anatole.'

'Good God!'

'You may well say "Good God!" You know what Anatole means to Tom.'

She did not need to labour the point. Uncle Tom combines a passionate love of food with a singular difficulty in digesting it, and Anatole is the only chef yet discovered who can fill him up to the Plimsoll mark without causing the worst sort of upheaval in his gastric juices.

'But would Anatole go to Runkle?'

'He'd go to anyone if the price was right.'

'None of that faithful old retainer stuff?'

'None. His outlook is entirely practical. That's the French in him.'

'I wonder you've been able to keep him so long. He must have had other offers.'

'I've always topped them. If it was simply another case of outbidding the opposition, I wouldn't be worrying.'

'But when Uncle Tom comes back and finds Anatole conspicuous by his absence, won't the home be a bit in the melting pot?'

'I don't like to think of it.'

But she did think of it. So did I. And we were both thinking of it, when our musings were interrupted by the return of L. P. Runkle, who waddled in and fixed us with a bulging eye.

I suppose if he had been slenderer, one might have described him as a figure of doom, but even though so badly in need of a reducing diet he was near enough to being one to make my interior organs do a quick shuffle-off-to-Buffalo as if some muscular hand had stirred them up with an egg-whisk. And when he began to speak, he was certainly impressive. These fellows who have built up large commercial empires are always what I have heard Jeeves call orotund. They get that way from dominating meetings of shareholders. Having started off with 'Oh, there you are, Mrs Travers', he went into his speech, and it was about as orotund as anything that has ever come my way. It ran, as nearly as I can remember, as follows:

'I was hoping to see you, Mrs Travers. In a previous conversation, you will recall that I stated uncompromisingly that your nephew Mr Wooster had purloined the silver porringer which I brought here to sell to your husband, whose absence I greatly deplore. That this was no mere suspicion has now been fully substantiated. I have a witness who is prepared to testify on oath in court that he found it in the top drawer of the chest of drawers in Mr Wooster's bedroom, unskilfully concealed behind socks and handkerchiefs.'

Here if it had been a shareholders meeting, he would probably have been reminded of an amusing story which may be new to some of you present this afternoon, but I suppose in a private conversation he saw no need for it. He continued, still orotund.

'The moment I report this to the police and acquaint them with the evidence at my disposal, Wooster's arrest will follow automatically, and a sharp sentence will be the inevitable result.'

It was an unpleasant way of putting it, but I was compelled to admit that it covered the facts like a bedspread. Dust off that cell, Wormwood Scrubs, I was saying to myself, I shall soon be with you.

'Such is the position. But I am not a vindictive man, I have no wish, if it can be avoided, to give pain to a hostess who has been to such trouble to make my visit enjoyable.'

He paused for a moment to lick his lips, and I knew he was tasting again those master-dishes of Anatole's. And it was on Anatole that he now touched.

'While staying here as your guest, I have been greatly impressed by the skill and artistry of your chef. I will agree not to press charges against Mr Wooster provided you consent to let this gifted man leave your employment and enter mine.'

A snort rang through the room, one of the ancestor's finest. You might almost have called it orotund. Following it with the word 'Ha!', she turned to me with a spacious wave of the hand.

'Didn't I tell you, Bertie? Wasn't I right? Didn't I say the child of unmarried parents would blackmail me?'

A fellow with the excess weight of L. P. Runkle finds it difficult to stiffen all over when offended, but he stiffened as far as he could. It was as if some shareholder at the meeting had said the wrong thing.

'Blackmail?'

'That's what I said.'

'It is not blackmail. It is nothing of the sort.'

'He is quite right, madam,' said Jeeves, appearing from nowhere. I'll swear he hadn't been there half a second before. 'Blackmail implies the extortion of money. Mr Runkle is merely extorting a cook.'

'Exactly. A purely business transaction,' said Runkle, obviously considering him a Daniel come to judgment.

'It would be very different,' said Jeeves, 'were somebody to try to obtain money from him by threatening to reveal that while in America he served a prison sentence for bribing a juror in a case in which he was involved.'

A cry broke from L. P. Runkle's lips, somewhat similar to the one the cat Gus had uttered when the bag of cat food fell on him. He tottered and his face would, I think, have turned ashy white if his blood pressure hadn't been the sort that makes it pretty tough going for a face to turn ashy white. The best it could manage was something Florence would have called sallow.

The ancestor, on the other hand, had revived like a floweret beneath the watering-can. Not that she looks like a floweret, but you know what I mean.

'What!' she ejaculated.

'Yes, madam, the details are all in the club book. Bingley recorded them very fully. His views were very far to the left at the time, and I think he derived considerable satisfaction from penning an exposé of a gentleman of Mr Runkle's wealth. It is also with manifest gusto that he relates how Mr Runkle, in grave danger of a further prison sentence in connection with a real estate fraud, forfeited the money he had deposited as security for his appearance in court and disappeared.'

'Jumped his bail, you mean?'

'Precisely, madam. He escaped to Canada in a false beard.'

The ancestor drew a deep breath. Her eyes were glowing more like twin stars than anything. Had not her dancing days been long past, I think she might have gone into a brisk buck-and-wing. The lower limbs twitched just as if she were planning to.

'Well,' she said, 'a nice bit of news that'll be for the fellows who dole out knighthoods. "Runkle?" they'll say. "That old lag? If we made a man like that a knight, we'd never hear the last of it. The boys on the Opposition benches would kid the pants off us." We were discussing, Runkle, yesterday that little matter of the money you ought to have given Tuppy Glossop years ago. If you will step into my boudoir, we will go into it again at our leisure.'

17

The following day dawned bright and clear, at least I
suppose it did, but I wasn't awake at the time. When
eventually I came to life, the sun was shining, all Nature
appeared to be smiling, and Jeeves was bringing in the
breakfast tray. Gus the cat, who had been getting his
eight hours on an adjacent armchair, stirred, opened an
eye and did a sitting high jump on to the bed, eager not
to miss anything that was going.

'Good morning, Jeeves.'

'Good morning, sir.'

'Weather looks all right.'

'Extremely clement, sir.'

'The snail's on the wing and the lark's on the thorn, or
rather the other way round, as I've sometimes heard you
say. Are those kippers I smell?'

'Yes, sir.'

'Detach a portion for Gus, will you. He will probably
like to take it from the soap dish, reserving the saucer
for milk.'

'Very good, sir.'

I sat up and eased the spine into the pillows. I was
conscious of a profound peace.

'Jeeves,' I said, 'I am conscious of a profound peace. I
wonder if you remember me telling you a few days ago
that I was having a sharp attack of euphoria?'

'Yes, sir. I recall your words clearly. You said you
were sitting on top of the world with a rainbow round
your shoulder.'

'Similar conditions prevail this morning. I thought
everything went off very well last night, didn't you?'

'Yes, sir.'

'Thanks to you.'

'It is very kind of you to say so, sir.'

'I take it the ancestor came to a satisfactory arrangement with Runkle?'

'Most satisfactory, sir. Madam has just informed me that Mr Runkle was entirely co-operative.'

'So Tuppy and Angela will be joined in holy wedlock, as the expression is?'

'Almost immediately, I understood from Madam.'

'And even now Ginger and M. Glendennon are probably in conference with the registrar of their choice.'

'Yes, sir.'

'And Spode has got a black eye, which one hopes is painful. In short, on every side one sees happy endings popping up out of traps. A pity that Bingley is flourishing like a green what-is-it, but one can't have everything.'

'No, sir. *Medio de fonte leporum surgit amari aliquid in ipsis floribus angat.*'

'I don't think I quite followed you there, Jeeves.'

'I was quoting from the Roman poet Lucretius, sir. A rough translation would be "From the heart of this fountain of delights wells up some bitter taste to choke them even among the flowers".'

'Who did you say wrote that?'

'Lucretius, sir, 99–55 BC.'

'Gloomy sort of bird.'

'His outlook was perhaps somewhat sombre, sir.'

'Still, apart from Bingley, one might describe joy as reigning supreme.'

'A very colourful phrase, sir.'

'Not my own. I read it somewhere. Yes, I think we may say everything's more or less oojah-cum-spiff. With one exception, Jeeves,' I said, a graver note coming into my voice as I gave Gus his second helping of kipper. 'There remains a fly in the ointment, a familiar saying

meaning . . . well, I don't quite know what it does mean.
It seems to imply a state of affairs at which one is
supposed to look askance, but why, I ask myself,
shouldn't flies be in ointment? What harm do they do?
And who wants ointment, anyway? But you get what
I'm driving at. The Junior Ganymede club book is still in
existence. That is what tempers my ecstasy with
anxiety. We have seen how packed with trinitrotoluol it
is, and we know how easily it can fall into the hands of
the powers of darkness. Who can say that another
Bingley may not come along and snitch it from the
secretary's room? I know it is too much to ask you to
burn the beastly thing, but couldn't you at least destroy
the eighteen pages in which I figure?'

'I have already done so, sir.'

I leaped like a rising trout, to the annoyance of Gus,
who had gone to sleep on my solar plexus. Words failed
me, but in due season I managed three.

'Much obliged, Jeeves.'

'Not at all, sir.'

The P G Wodehouse Society (UK)

The P G Wodehouse Society (UK) was formed in 1997 and exists to promote the enjoyment of the works of the greatest humorist of the twentieth century.

The Society publishes a quarterly magazine, *Wooster Sauce*, which features articles, reviews, archive material and current news. It also publishes an occasional newsletter in the *By The Way* series which relates a single matter of Wodehousean interest. Members are rewarded in their second and subsequent years by receiving a specially produced text of a Wodehouse magazine story which has never been collected into one of his books.

A variety of Society events are arranged for members including regular meetings at a London club, a golf day, a cricket match, a Society dinner, and walks round Bertie Wooster's London. Meetings are also arranged in other parts of the country.

Membership enquiries

Membership of the Society is available to applicants from all parts of the world. The cost of a year's membership in 1998 was £15. Enquiries and requests for an application form should be addressed in writing to the Membership Secretary, Helen Murphy, at 16 Herbert Street, Plaistow, London E13 8BE, or write to the Editor of *Wooster Sauce*, Tony Ring, at 34 Longfield Road, Great Missenden, Bucks HP16 0EG.

You can visit their website at:
http://www.eclipse.co.uk/wodehouse